"Please don't put my father in jail."

Devon hated pleading, but she was desperate. "Prison would kill him...and he didn't take the money for himself. The debt is mine."

Grant looked at her arrogantly over his desk, his tone as cold as his eyes. "So when are *you* going to repay me?"

"Repay you...?"

"You said the debt was yours...."

"I'll work," she interjected before he had finished speaking. "I'll work hard for you... I'll do anything....."

"Good," he said, and he took his time before slowly drawling, "When can you move in?"

She knew what he meant, but she denied it to herself. He said relentlessly, "Make up your mind, Devon. Does your father go to prison... or do you come to live with me?"

Books by Jessica Steele

These books may be available at your local bookseller.

For a free catalog listing all titles currently available,
send your name and address to:

Harlequin Reader Service
P.O. Box 52040, Phoenix, AZ 85072-2040
Canadian address: Stratford, Ontario N5A 6W2

Tomorrow— Come Soon

Jessica Steele

Harlequin Books

TORONTO • NEW YORK • LONDON
AMSTERDAM • PARIS • SYDNEY • HAMBURG
STOCKHOLM • ATHENS • TOKYO • MILAN

Original hardcover edition published in 1983
by Mills & Boon Limited

ISBN 0-373-02607-2

Harlequin Romance first edition March 1984

CHAPTER ONE

DEVON closed the lid on the last of her packing, wishing at the same time that she could as easily pull the lid down on the excitement that was building up in her. She had been bitterly disappointed before.

But nothing was going to go wrong this time. She had to be convinced of that she thought, as her beautiful blue eyes went slowly round her bedroom which after tomorrow she would not be seeing for another two months—if all went well. And it *had* to go well.

She had been aware for some time now that she was going more and more into herself, hating the times she had to leave the walls of the small detached house she shared with her only relative, her father.

Her thoughts stayed on her father as she considered that never would she be able to repay him for his love and caring this past six years, nor for the understanding he had shown for her every mood more recently.

She owed him so much, not least for his patience and tact on those black days when to so much as leave the house to go as far as the corner shop for some small item was beyond her. Her father worked in a top position in the finance department of Harrington Enterprises, the largest employer in the sizeable town of Marchworth where they lived. He was well respected in his job, and because of his trusted position in the firm, was well paid for the work he did. And if he had taken it on himself to collect the major supplies for the house, saying, 'I can get the shopping on my way home, if you like,' when he knew that though not being able to carry anything heavy she could have managed with the shopping trolley he had bought her, then that was one more indication of his tact. Because although she had never said, he had understood that she just hated going into the centre of town where it seemed that all eyes were watching her.

Devon crossed the floor of her room, her mind still on her father and how she was going to try and make it up to him when she came back from Sweden and everything was all right again. Excitement and hope burned in her. Everything was going to be all right; it had got to be. She just would not be able to bear it if at the end of it all she was just the same as she was now.

One shoulder dipping to one side, she limped ponderously down the stairs, her imagination going wild as she pictured herself months from now running down those same stairs; with no need to hang grimly on to the bannister rail for fear with each step that her right hip might let her down and that she would go crashing to the bottom.

Charles Johnston, a man of fifty-two with a shock of prematurely white hair, put down his paper as she limped into the sitting-room, the brilliant blue of his eyes noting the light of anticipation in those same brilliant blue eyes his daughter had inherited.

'All packed?' he enquired, his mouth showing his ever present smile of encouragement for her.

Devon nodded. 'Oh, Dad, I can't believe it! It—it seems like a dream that not only have you found this Dr Henekssen in Sweden who says he can correct . . .' she faltered, '. . . my—my hip—but that you've found the money so that I can have the operation.' Tears shone in her eyes as she told him, 'I shall never be out of your debt.'

Not an outwardly emotional man, he cleared his throat. Devoted to his daughter, he knew more than anyone what this operation meant to her. He, more than anyone, had seen the effect the motor accident had had on the lively fifteen-and-a-half-year-old she had been. His wife had died in the accident, and part of Devon becoming more and more withdrawn had been attributed at the time to her losing her mother at such an important time in her growing up. But she had undergone two operations that had left her still with that ungainly limp she so hated, and he had watched as she reached the age of twenty-one and had seen that, suffering the loss of her mother as she undoubtedly had, there was still no sign of her returning to the happy-go-lucky girl she had been before the accident.

'The money is yours, not mine,' he reminded her, adding gruffly, 'All I want from you is to see you happy.'

He refrained from saying what was in his mind, that nothing would give him greater pleasure than to see her mixing with other young people of her own age. For, not caring to know anyone of her own age group, preferring as she did not to let anyone see what to her over the years had become a hideous deformity, Devon had no friends.

'I'll go and get your cases down,' he said, leaving his seat. 'It will save time in the morning. You have an early start, remember.'

She beamed one of her rare smiles at him, the hope in her heart again that tomorrow would be the last time she would limp out of the house.

Her father left the room, and as she heard him on his way upstairs, she was hating that any other twenty-one-and-a-half-year-old would have been able to carry her own suitcases down the stairs, and would not have had to leave it to her parent. Not that he was ancient. He was quite spritely on his feet, even though she sometimes thought he deliberately slowed down his steps when she was around because of the wide contrast in their movements.

She had tried so hard not to let him see how down she often felt, for he too had scars from the accident. Not that he had been injured, but he had loved her mother dearly, and it had been he who had been driving at the time. He hadn't been responsible for the accident, but she knew he tortured himself still with the 'if's' of could he possibly have avoided the collision when an inebriated driver had come from nowhere and crashed into them.

With both of them nursing scars, it had been by un-spoken mutual consent that neither of them spoke of the accident to outsiders. The money received from the insur-ance company had soon been swallowed up by specialists' bills and treatment, and they had moved to a smaller house. And so far as any of their present neighbours knew, though they had little to do with any of them, the way Devon walked was the result of something she had been born with.

Devon heard her father come down and put her cases in the hall. She was too churned up to want to eat, but she eased herself up from the settee where she was sitting, and waited the necessary seconds until she was sure she had her balance. Then she limped out, calling as she passed him, 'I'm making you a special dinner tonight, since you'll be eating your own ghastly cooking from tomorrow.'

Her good humour remained with her throughout the meal, her mind full of all she had to look forward to; not to mention, pray God, that in a couple of months she would be able to carry her own suitcases.

'I'll make it up to you, Dad,' she said suddenly, chokily, making his eyes lift quickly from his favourite chocolate soufflé which she had laboured over.

'Make what up, child?' he enquired quietly, his eyes on her flushed face, sensing she was on the verge of talking about a subject she was more prone to want to leave in some dark corner.

'All the time and money you've spent on me,' she said, awash with gratitude. 'I—know it hasn't been easy and—and I must have kept you permanently broke in getting the best specialists as you have. You must have spent no end in trying to find someone prepared to have another try.'

'Rubbish,' he said stoutly. 'You had to finish growing before another attempt could be made on you anyway. And anyhow, we had a new car last year, didn't we?'

'A new secondhand one,' she replied, cloud coming to her eyes as she remembered that the car that had been written off in the accident had been a new model that year. 'You could have used some of that money from that endowment policy to buy a new one,' she reminded him.

'But we already had a car by then,' he in turn reminded her. 'And anyway, the money from that policy is yours by right. I explained all that to you when out of the blue we heard that the policy had matured.'

Devon was silent as her mind went back to some six months ago. She had been particularly down just then, she recalled. Her twenty-first birthday had come and gone and her thoughts had dwelt on the fact that surely by now she had finished growing, but that even if there was someone in the world who could perform the miracle of surgery to make her whole, the appearance of a secondhand car decreed that her father would just not be able to afford it.

As she had at eighteen, at twenty-one she had refused to have a birthday party. Who would she invite anyway? They knew no one.

Yes, she had been lower then than at any time, Devon remembered. And the thing was, although she was aware of her father's worried glances in her direction, she had just seemed incapable of shaking herself out of it. Those had been really bad days, days when she had led a hermit-like existence simply because she couldn't face going out.

And then one day, about three weeks after her twenty-first birthday, her father had come home with two pieces of truly unbelievable news. The first, that he had been making enquiries for some time now about the possibility of a third operation for her, and how he had heard of a man in Sweden who had performed several similar operations before—all with a successful outcome.

The depression that had encased her had started to crack. But that was before she realised that the Swedish surgeon might as well have his clinic on the moon for all the chance she had of getting to him.

'I'm—glad for those other people he's operated on,' she had managed, forcing a smile in the face of her father's look of expecting her to be overjoyed.

'Be glad for yourself, Devon,' he had said. 'You're going to have that operation too, child.'

Her heart had lifted, joy wanting to surge, part of her wanting her father to make any sacrifice for her—but then she discovered that she couldn't let him; she must keep her joy in check.

'You've sacrificed enough . . .'

But he had cut in, explaining that he didn't have to sacrifice a thing. Telling her that for years he had been paying premiums on an endowment in her name that was due for payment when she reached twenty-one, and that because the premiums were paid by standing order, he had forgotten all about it until that day he had received some correspondence from the insurance company concerned.

'An endowment?' Devon had cried her astonishment. 'In my name?'

'Paying in for years by the same method, I forgot all about it,' he repeated, going on, 'I've made some enquiries and it will be just enough for you to go to Sweden.'

'On my own?' she had enquired, never having been far from her parent's side, then that fact was getting mixed up with the growing wonder, the daring to believe what it was he was saying!

'I'd only be able to visit you for limited periods if I came with you,' he said practically. And there was a coaxing note in his voice she didn't really need as the fantastic chance that was within her grasp began to sink in. 'I'll take you to the airport, of course, and meet you when you come back.'

Slow tears began to trickle down her face. 'Oh—Dad!' It was all she was capable of saying.

Her trip to Sweden, they discovered, was not to be immediate. But after five and a half years of having a hip which often never quite knew how to behave itself, Devon was to find the months that followed, while her medical consultant, Mr McAllen, exchanged letters and forwarded X-rays to Sweden, the most trying and frustrating of all. But hope was in her heart too. And if during those waiting months she occasionally paused to wonder how, with her father daily working with figures as he kept a watchful eye on the incomings and outgoings of Grant Harrington's company finances, he should then be so mindless of his own incomings and outgoings to forget the periodic outgoings from his own account in the shape of payments on her endowment—hefty payments they must have been too, to yield the amount they had—then these thoughts did not settle for long enough to worry her. Her mind would soon spin on to her future post-operative days, to the freedom of movement that could be hers, to the time, dare she believe it, when she would be going to her first dance!

Charles Johnston had a second helping of chocolate soufflé, then pushed back his chair from the table to start stacking a tray ready to carry their used dishes back to the kitchen.

'You've got a long day in front of you tomorrow,' he told Devon. 'I'll wash up. I should have an early night if I were you.'

'I'm going to fuss over you when I come home,' she teased, too fearful of the dark despair that would be hers to think about coming home with no improvement. 'But since you'll be doing your own washing up for a while, I'll do it tonight.'

The washing up completed, Devon knew she was far too excited to sleep. Besides which, having been in hospital before, she knew she was going to be heartily sick and tired of lying in bed before she was through.

She guessed her father had read her thoughts when instead of heading for the stairs after leaving the kitchen, she went into the sitting room. He followed her in, his step slow, used as he was not to give her the impression that her slow progress hindered his own smarter pace.

Automatically she made for the settee. It was where she always sat, or, if her hip was nagging, lay with her feet up. Her father took his usual chair, but made no move to switch on the television. They both knew, full of hope, that after tonight the tenor of their lives would be different.

Many times during the past months, Devon had been near to discussing her career prospects with her parent. If everything went well, and she just couldn't think about failure, then it was more than time she did something to repay the colossal sums he had paid out on her behalf. But just when she was about to make her first positive statement about her working, suddenly there was a ring at the front door, and her positive thinking hurriedly departed.

Who could be calling? Seldom was it that anyone came to the door! She hated meeting strangers, hated anyone to see her the way she was.

'I'll go,' said Charles Johnston, an unnecessary statement since she hadn't moved. Their eyes met and as he went to the sitting room door, he gave her a reassuring smile that she read as telling her not to worry, that whoever it was, he would not be inviting them in.

For a minute or so as she heard voices at the door, she was reassured. She was half sitting, half lying with her feet up on the settee, her shoes on the floor beside her, security wrapped around her. Soon, she knew, she would hear the door close on whoever it was out there.

But her feeling of security was doomed not to last. For the front door had closed—yet she could still hear voices! Whoever it was had been invited *in*! And not only that— her father was bringing whoever it was into the sitting room!!

The door handle to the room turned, and there just wasn't time for her to make the laborious adjustment needed to bring her feet over the side of the settee. Which left her, when the door swung inwards, looking like a perfectly healthy young woman who was lounging languidly about, while her white-haired father went back and forth to answer every summons at the door.

Composing herself as best she could, knowing that her impairment could not possibly be seen while she remained where she was—and she had no intention of moving—her eyes went past her father, who for once was absentminded about her, and on to the tall man who filled the doorway just behind him.

It struck her then that their visitor had to be someone important. Why else would her father invite in someone who, in the flick of a glance he threw her way, gave her the feeling he had in that dark glance computerised her pale almost translucent skin, her wavy gossamer soft blonde hair, and the rest of her? Why, if he wasn't important, had her father brought the thirty-five or thirty-six-year-old man into the best room when he knew that she, she with her aversion to meeting stangers, would be there?

As the man followed her father into the room, so her father frowned and seemed to come to, to realise she was there and that his manners were at fault.

'This—is Mr Harrington,' he introduced the unsmiling man, confirming for her that their visitor *was* someone very important if he was *Grant* Harrington. 'My daughter Devon,' he was completing, as her mind went on to decide that since Harrington senior had died some years before, then this man had to be the boss of the multi-million-pound empire for whom her father worked.

Knowing Mr Harrington would have to take a few strides to reach her, and that it could only look rude that she wasn't getting to her feet to meet him halfway, Devon did what she could in the way of politeness by offering him the best she could in the way of a smile, and extended her hand, her voice husky from sudden nerves if he should take offence, as she said:

'How do you do.'

To be ignored, to have her hand ignored when she had expected it to be taken in the brief formality of a handshake, jolted her. And she was further jolted to discover that Mr Harrington after that first computerised glance, needed no other, it seemed, to sum her up and file her away as beneath his notice. Very often she had been aware of people staring at her—through the way she walked—but never had she met anyone who had looked straight through her!

Her hand fell back to the settee, tension taking a grip on her. To her mind, tension was filling the air, although the tall man seemed unaware of it. She glanced quickly to her father and saw that she wasn't alone in feeling tense. He was looking quite dreadful, she thought, and had to know then how much he cared for her, as she guessed he was cursing his forgetfulness in bringing a stranger in—his terribly worried look, all on account of how on edge he knew she would be feeling.

'Can I—get you a drink, Grant?' he asked jerkily, corroborating what her senses had already fixed in her mind. This dark-haired, dark-eyed man just had to be boss.

The offer of a drink was ignored. Which was just as well, she thought, since he didn't look the sherry type, and sherry was all they had in. Though she felt a niggle of something akin to anger, foreign in her, that he should brush her father's civil attempt to play host aside, and question:

'I noticed suitcases in the hall—which one of you is going away?' Perhaps he was trying to be civil after all, she thought. But neither she nor her father had answered him, when he asked crisply, 'Or are both of you taking a trip?'

The question perhaps was not such an odd one. Her father knew all there was to know about high finance and could be missed if he was taking a holiday at an inconvenient time. But she guessed when he seemed struck dumb that, too honest to lie to his employer, he was protecting her by not answering. She saw then that it was up to her to make the reply, and from her indolent position she spoke up in place of her father, her voice husky still as she reasoned that Grant Harrington would never glean why it was she was going away.

'It's me, actually,' she said, forcing another smile. 'I'm going to Stockholm tomorrow.'

She had thought he considered her beneath his notice, but she had drawn stern dark eyes to her, and she wished she had stayed quiet. She saw he was looking angry suddenly, or maybe he always looked that way.

'From the size of your luggage, you appear ready for an extended holiday,' he remarked curtly.

Devon hardly thought that 'holiday' would cover what she had let herself in for. But at being reminded that tomorrow was the start of something that could mean so much, she forgot that she must be giving Grant Harrington the impression that she loved the easy life, and could not help that excitement should start to stir in her again. Or that that excitement should show in the sparkle that came to her eyes as she looked at him, as her mouth curved, and knowing her father wouldn't breathe a word of why she was going, she smiled and said, a breathlessness in her voice:

'I'll see how I like it first—but I may stay a couple of months.'

Her father clearing his throat brought her back to realise that perhaps she was going a little over the top. Though she hadn't exactly lied to his employer either. If the operation was unsuccessful, and she just wasn't going to dwell on that, then she could be back home much sooner than the two months it would otherwise take.

The small coughing noise her father made drew Grant Harrington's attention away from her. She had gathered anyway that he had formed an opinion that, by the sound of it, she liked a good time and that too had been filed away, and unless she spoke again she wouldn't get spoken to.

Though she did think he could have dressed up a bit the blunt, 'I'd like a private word with you, Charles,' with which he addressed her father—effectively cutting her out as he added, obviously by now not expecting her to shift herself, 'Is there another room we could use?'

Devon saw her father was looking tense still, and she wanted to tell him that she didn't mind. 'Use the dining room, Dad,' she said, and smiled; for one of those rare occasions she was the one—to try to be reassuring. 'I think I'll go up to bed,' she added, her smile broadening at the secret they shared, a secret Grant Harrington was not privy too. 'Tomorrow is a big day,' she beamed.

She knew her father would be translating the message she had sent to mean that she would be making tracks to her room as soon as she had heard the dining room door close. And she knew he had got the translation right when, apparently not noticing that Grant Harrington had no word of 'goodnight' for her, her father left the sitting room door open as he and his visitor went out.

She was up in her room, having gone up the stairs as quickly as the pain in her hip would allow, just in case it was only a brief private word with her father that the head of Harrington's was after, but her mind was full of the two men downstairs.

Grant Harrington had never called at the house before, she mused as she got into bed, so perhaps something important was happening at Harringtons. How little she knew of the work her father did, she realised then. He had a top job, she knew that, but he wasn't a director or anything like that.

Perhaps Grant Harrington, knowing how extremely good her father was with figures, was contemplating a merger or a take-over or something and had only just heard that he wouldn't be in the office tomorrow? Take-overs didn't wait—he would have to see him tonight. Her father wouldn't have told anyone why he wanted the day off, or where he was going, she could be sure of that. Sure that none of his colleagues would know that he was taking her to the airport tomorrow.

Her pride in her father and his ability swelled as she saw the reason for Grant Harrington, after having seen her cases, curtly questioning which once of them was going away. He wouldn't want her father going on holiday if there was a take-over in the air. He would need him. Devon could understand him wanting their discussions to be in private too—from what she had read, those sort of things had to be very hush-hush. Something to do with a sudden rise in share prices, she rather thought.

Pride for her father took another upsurge that his position in the firm must be such that he should know all about the take-over. Grant Harrington thought a lot of him, that much was obvious.

As it was equally obvious, she thought, that Grant Harrington had no regard at all for her. She nibbled at her bottom lip as she reflected that she hadn't liked someone coming in and taking such an instant dislike to her. Oh, why hadn't he called in two months' time when she would be able to spring to her feet to shake hands with him, instead of being draped there like some wet lettuce looking as though she considered it too much of an effort to take a step off the settee to greet her father's employer.

She hadn't missed the arrogant look down his nose at her either at her admission, in this day and age when most people were eager to have a job, that she might be away for two months if she fancied it. She had earned herself another black mark by giving him the impression that she preferred to be one of life's pleasure-seekers—her father left to foot the bill whenever she felt like flitting off. No wonder he hadn't bothered about whether it was polite to come into her home and then promptly shut her out by asking to have a private word with her father.

She drifted into a light troubled sleep. But the sound of the front door closing had her coming wide awake. She felt easier knowing that Grant Harrington was out of her home. And when later she heard her father coming to bed, she flicked on her table lamp and called to him.

'Trouble at t'mill?' she enquired when he popped his head round the door.

'Nothing for you to worry your pretty head about,' he replied. 'It's time you were asleep.'

'Yes, Father,' she teased. Then urgently, the thought pushing itself to the front of her mind, 'You didn't tell Grant Harrington about my—my hip, did you?'

He came further into the room, ever aware of her selfconsciousness where her hip was concerned. 'You know me better than that, child,' he said gently.

'Sorry, Dad,' she apologised, and was once more on an even keel.

Though before she settled down to sleep again, she was to remember the affectionate way her father had told her not to worry her pretty head. Was she pretty? Did—did Grant Harrington think she was pretty?

She saw him again in her mind's eye, tall and large with a physique that wouldn't tolerate an ounce of fat, and she couldn't help but think that a woman would have to be more than pretty to gain his notice. Only beautiful women would get a second look from the virile-looking Grant Harrington, she felt sure.

She was tempted to get out of bed and take stock of her fine boned face. Then she remembered tomorrow, and wondered why she should have a sudden yen to be beautiful.

Rats to Grant Harrington, she thought. It would be more than enough if she could just walk straight—Oh, tomorrow, please come soon!

CHAPTER TWO

THERE was an inner elation about the girl who stood with her cases outside Marchworth railway station waiting for a taxi that Thursday. She was nearly at her journey's end, and had been hard put to it throughout that journey to keep that elation down. Hard put to it not to break out into a grin that would be misconstrued by the donors of every admiring glance that had come her way. And there had been a good few glances of admiration, she recalled.

But she was not interested in flirting, of responding to come-hither looks. Perhaps later she might enter into some lighthearted flirtation. She admitted that her education had been sadly lacking in that department. But for the moment all she wanted to do was to get home. To get home to her father. Elation bubbled again as she thought of her father and of showing him how well the money from that endowment had been spent.

Perhaps she had been just a wee bit selfish to spend what little money there was over on the smart, up-to-the-minute suit she had on, not to mention the, to her, absolutely adorable, for all they were quite plain, black three-inch-high-heeled shoes. At the moment the shoes were in her flight bag, but the instant she was in the taxi, she intended that they should change places with the flat ones she had on.

Happiness bubbled up as a taxi swung into the station forecourt, and a smile she could do nothing to hold back beamed from her as the taxi driver enquired, 'Where to, love?' Devon gave him her address, and giggled for the first time in what seemed years to hear his reply of, 'With a smile like that, I'll take you there for free!'

He didn't mean it, of course, but his remark did nothing to take from her the heady feeling that dominated her being. Perhaps being drunk was like this, she thought, as she unzipped her flight bag and took out the shoes that meant so much to her. Her first high heels!

Though she discounted that being drunk could feel like this. Her mind wasn't befuddled. She had clear remembrance of everything that had led up to this feeling of utter, sublime, elation.

There had been pain after the operation—and fear. Fear had grown into terror that to feel so much pain must mean that the surgery to her hip had not been successful.

Disbelief had followed when, after only three days, firm-armed, kind-hearted nursing staff had come to lift her out of bed. After that she had spent two days in just sitting out of bed and getting used to the idea that her days of being bed-bound were over.

And then had come the hard work of the physiotherapist. The hard work of the rest of the staff. Devon had worked hard too in learning to walk again, in learning to climb stairs. But oh, the rewards for that hard work, to find with breath-holding unbelievability, and utter, utter joy, that she was walking! That she was *actually* walking without that terribly ugly sideways lurch!

She had cried, Devon remembered. And she had laughed. Laughter and tears had mixed, so that Ingrid, her special nurse, unforgivably she told her afterwards, had shed a tear too.

Dr Henekssen had monitored her progress throughout. It was he who had given her the all-clear to leave his clinic.

'I can go *next* week!' she had exclaimed, when he had pronounced with a twinkle in his clever grey eyes, that reluctantly they would have to let her go after only seven weeks.

'Had you a home here in Sweden, I would have discharged you earlier when you could have attended my outpatients clinic,' he told her in his perfect English. 'But as it is, I wish to do the final check on you myself. Next week I think will be the right time.'

After that, next week had seemed a long time in coming. She had heard regularly from her father. But it was because in his last letter he had mentioned something about an air traffic controllers' strike at the airports, that she did not contact him to tell him she would be arriving home a week early. His disappointment, she knew, would be as great as hers if she couldn't get home when expected. And remembering her own seemingly endless wait, she didn't want to occupy one of Dr Henekssen's beds a minute longer when the day came and he said she could go. To this end she was busy making contingency plans to stay in a modest hotel if she had to stay on in Sweden for any length of time after leaving the clinic.

The day of her final check-up at last arrived. But she had known a few anxious moments when Dr Henekssen had told her that she must report to her consultant in England some six weeks hence.

'Something has gone wrong!' she had gasped, appalled. 'Something . . .'

'No, no,' he had said quickly to soothe her fears.

'But you said this was to be my final check . . .'

'Your final check here, I should have said. It is a perfectly normal arrangement. Had you been resident in Stockholm I would have seen you myself in six weeks' time.' And he had smiled, and teased, 'You walk without a limp, do you not?'

'Yes,' she had agreed. And her gratitude to him was boundless as she had then apologised for her fears, and he had gone on to tell her that she had not one single thing to fear provided she was sensible.

'Sensible?' she had queried. And she had vowed to be sensible for the little while longer he had requested of her. In a while, he had said, she would be able to do anything she had ever wanted to do. But first she must watch not to overtire or overstrain that hip. Though she should exercise, she should not put too much stress on that part of her that was knitting well together. If she took heed of his advice, if she took care to rest frequently as well as to exercise, then her visit to Mr McAllen in six weeks' time would be a mere formality, no more. Dr Henekssen's final advice, that maybe she should leave it until after she had seen Mr McAllen before she tackled a ten-mile hike, had made her laugh.

And she had been laughing inside ever since. The strike over, she'd had little trouble in booking her flight home. And though she could have telephoned her father to meet her at the airport as they had agreed he would do, by then the delicious idea of walking in unannounced, of walking in, not limping in, to show him the good-as-new Devon Johnston, had taken a hold of her.

She had spent two nights in a hotel, and had time to purchase her suit and shoes, and she thought, as the taxi drew up outside her home, there could not be a happier girl in the whole of England.

So happy was she, she was oblivious to the fact that the taxi driver had to pull up some distance ahead of her gate. A long sleek car was in the way.

'Here you are, love,' he said as he put down her cases on the pavement. 'It seems a shame to take your money.'

She laughed with him, and handed him a large tip. Soon she would get a job, and anyway, the way she felt, what did money matter? Her tip had him offering to take her cases up to the door for her, and remembering the doctor's advice on her being sensible, Devon almost let him. But in having lost her limp, there was a new-found independence surging in her. It was more than high time she learned to do things for herself, was her considered opinion. She refused his offer, still not yet over the fantastic feeling of being able to get to her feet and moving off without first having to wait until she had her balance.

Her father had not heard her arrive, that was for sure, she thought, as on the front door step she contemplated ringing the door bell and giving him a surprise that way. But it was dark now, and she wanted to have full view of the delight on his face when he saw her.

She rummaged in her bag for her door key, and leaving her cases to the side of the porch, silently she let herself in. She saw the line of light showing beneath the sitting room door, and her heart was ready to burst, for she knew that that was where she would find him.

Her hand was on the sitting room door, when a smile of mischief widened her mouth. In the next second she had the door open, and in a swirl of activity she was pirouetting into the room, her cry of 'Tar-rah!' breaking off as pain assaulted her hip, and she lost her balance and went cannoning into the hard unmovable figure standing there.

The pain in her hip frightened her, and had scorching fears returning that she was back to having to get her balance before she moved. She clutched tightly on to her father, who oddly, seemed to have grown in stature in her absence, while she tried to best her panic.

Panic faded, and with it pain, as she sorted out that with her hip still healing, and with her feet unaccustomed to their new high heels, neither was ready yet for such a crazy spin into the room.

And then the figure she had been clutching on to as though to life was pushing her roughly away. And Devon was gasping afresh, though this time not in pain, for she found she had perfect balance, but from shock. For the large man she had grabbed hold of was, she now saw, very different in build and height from what he should be. He was, in fact, not her father at all!

Shock to see she had launched herself at the self-same man who had visited her father on her last night at home left her dumb for several seconds.

But not so the man she had seen only once, though she had never forgotten him—seven weeks in hospital had left her with a lot of time at her disposal. And she was soon to discover that in those seven weeks she had been gone, his liking for her had not gone up at all. For there was aggression added to the none too polite way he had treated her before.

'You're back in England,' he reminded her grittily. 'Back where a parental eye might be kept on you—don't come the free love tricks you've been practising in Stockholm with me.'

Free love! Good heavens, was that what he thought she had gone to Sweden for—to do as she wished without her father there to check her? Speechless from what he had said, Devon stared at him.

She watched his eyes travel disparagingly down over her new suit, his unflattering appraisal reaching her trim ankles and dainty feet, before he lifted hard eyes to study her pale face. She felt tired suddenly, when tiredness had been kept at bay by the elation she had thought she would never lose but which, all at once, she had. She guessed that tiredness was showing in her face as Grant Harrington's lips curved cynically as though he was putting his own interpretation on why she should arrive back looking done in, from what he obviously considered the free love capital of the world.

Struggling out of fresh shock that any man could say such things to her, Devon managed to find her voice.

'Wh-where is my father?' she questioned, her voice having a husky quality, and nowhere as firm as she would have liked to have heard it.

Her question was ignored as she found herself in for some more of his insolent scrutiny as, his expression sardonic, he did not give her a straightforward reply, which was all she wanted, but answered sneeringly:

'Fancy you remembering you have one. You cut your holiday short by one week—didn't Sweden come up to expectations?'

Nothing wrong with his mental arithmetic—his manner had flushed out that stranger to her of anger. And Devon was glad of it. For it replaced the shock she felt that he was seeing her as totally as something she was not, and made her forget entirely that he was her father's employer.

'You'll never know what Sweden can do for a girl,' she told him shortly—and was ready then to go looking herself for her father, since it looked as though insults were all she could expect if she stayed where she was.

'I can take a good guess.' He was having the last word as his eyes flicked again over her suit, an intimation there she couldn't miss, that without a doubt she had got some poor Swedish sucker to pay for it.

Angry words flared near to the surface. But just in time, memory came that the only possible reason he could be in her home had to be because of something to do with the company her father worked for. She remembered that the most detestable man she had ever had the misfortune to meet was her father's employer.

'You'll excuse me, Mr Har . . .' she started to say stiffly, but broke off as she heard footsteps.

She turned her back on Grant Harrington as those footsteps neared. And she had her eyes on the doorway when the smaller man came through it, then stood stock-still, looking at her as if he just could not believe his eyes.

It was her father who stood there—and yet not her father. The man who had halted at the sight of her; the man who stood blinking as though he thought her some sort of mirage—had aged ten years in the short time she had been away!

'Dad!' she cried.

And then it was as if some magic had whisked those added ten years away. Nobody watching could miss seeing his unbounded delight as Devon moved the several steps up to him, not a sign of a limp, a lurch, about her.

She forgot all about Grant Harrington being there. Forgot that he was watching the way her father, his delight immense at the physical change in her, put his arms around her and hugged her as though she had been away a year. She was mindless that to an outsider who knew nothing of why this homecoming should be so joyous, it should seem she looked to be an adored daughter who had been away much too long. She was too busy battling against tears to think about him—tears had no part in this happy homecoming.

Charles Johnston, too, was for the moment oblivious of the other man. 'Why didn't you let me know you were coming home? I would have come to the airport to meet you,' he said, and his eyes were shining too as, with the memory of that stab of pain, this time Devon did a sedate twirl around for him.

She was sure they would have hugged each other again from sheer gladness, had not a harsh voice cut in abruptly:

'You have the keys, Charles?'

At that moment Devon felt she hated Grant Harrington that his cold harsh voice should intrude on this time of happy reunion. But as she looked from her father to the stern glacier features of the taller man, and back again to her father—so a new fear entered her heart. And it was a fear that had nothing at all to do with the success or otherwise of her operation.

For her father was suddenly looking old again. That shining light had gone from his eyes, and as he moved from her towards his employer, she knew just then, without having to be told, that something very, very dreadful had happened while she was away.

Choking back comment, she watched, her eyes widening, as she saw her father hand over keys which she knew were his office keys because of the key-ring they hung from. A key-ring she herself had bought him when he had complained about the office keys getting mixed up with his home set.

Neither man had anything to say. The keys were taken without thanks. And as, bewildered, Devon searched for a reason why her father's employer should so sternly be taking the office key, the safe key, and other keys that had been in her father's possession for as long as she could remember, Grant Harrington did say something, the effect of which made her father's face go a putty sort of grey.

'I'll be in touch,' he clipped, and made a movement indicating that there was nothing more to be said, that he wanted to be off.

'I'll—see you out,' Charles Johnston replied, finding his voice, mindless that Devon was staring at them both as she tried to grasp what it was all about.

Stunned to see her father with his proud head bent as he preceded his employer from the room, she came to life as Grant Harrington, with neither word nor look for her, would have followed him.

'What's going on?' she addressed his back.

He looked set to ignore her, but her feelings were all for her father, and she wasn't having that. With a speed new to her, Devon flew to grab hold of his arm, catching him in the doorway.

Hostilely he turned round, his eyes going to look distastefully down at her hand on the immaculate sleeve of his suit jacket.

'What's happen . . .' she began, before his arrogant stare had her taking her hand from him.

'Pretending you don't know, Miss Johnston?' he bit cynically.

'I don't kn . . .'

'There's nothing your father wouldn't do for you, is there?' he sliced through her denial, his voice a seething undertone. 'I've seen with my own eyes that he worships the ground you walk on.' And while she had started to gape, contempt blazed from him as he tore into her furiously, 'The trouble with women like you is that somebody else always has to pay the price. It's *you*, you idle bitch, who has brought your father to this dishonour!'

'Dis—honour!' she exclaimed hoarsely, fresh shock making her voice barely audible.

But he had heard it, and was straight away discounting any truth in the roundness of her eyes. 'You can throw away your passport,' he informed her brutishly, 'your jet-setting days are over.'

'Jet . . . ?' She still wasn't with him.

'The horn of plenty has just dried up,' he said succinctly.

And with that she was staring at his back as he strode purposefully to the front door. With only the briefest of nods at her father, he strode out into the night.

Devon stood where Grant Harrington had left her, the words he had uttered spinning crazily around in her head. She watched without really seeing the way her father, used as he was to carrying anything heavy for her, having spotted her suitcases in the porch was mechanically bringing them into the hall.

He straightened up. But it was when he wouldn't meet

her eyes that the words 'horn of plenty', that word 'dishonour', changed from merely spinning to start roaring in
her ears. And she was then going forward, an arm going
round him protectively. And she just had to ask:

'Did—did an—endowment really pay for my—operation?'

Fifteen minutes later, not sure who had supported
whom as they had moved from the hall and back into the
sitting room, Devon was still not believing what her
parent had confessed in answer to the question she had
not really expected a denial to.

Her father's honour was without question. She knew it,
just as everyone else knew it. His employer knew it too,
was certain of it, why else did he have such a trusted
position?

But even when, no joy about him now to have his
good-as-new daughter home, Charles Johnston leaned his
head back against his chair and closed his eyes for some
seconds, even then Devon could not believe it.

'You'll have to know, child. You'd guess anyway before
too long when I no longer got the car out to go to the office.
It was Grant Harrington, or rather his company, who
paid for you to have that operation.'

For how long she sat numbed, Devon couldn't have
said. Then, her mind darting up all channels, she opened
her mouth, and closed it again. It appeared to her then
that anything she thought to say would come out sounding like an accusation.

She valued honesty every bit as much as her father, but
whatever he had done, he had not done it for himself.
Blame there was. But not blame down to him. It was her
blame. Only now was she beginning to see what a pathetic
creature she had been. She had not been exactly brim-
ming over with acceptance of her fate, had she?

'Oh, Dad,' she said softly, wanting, needing to help him

in what must be a terrible time for him. Harrington's as the loser had ceased to exist in her mind just then. All she could think of was her father, and what his pride, his self-respect must be suffering at this moment. 'You— didn't expect to be found out?' she enquired gently, tentatively, instinct telling her it would be better for him if she could get him to talk about it.

He looked at her, and quickly away, making her feel dreadful that he should be too ashamed to meet her eyes, when everything he had ever done had all been for her. Then he coughed, and cleared his throat, and then as if it was being dragged from him, he began:

'I thought—I'd been exceptionally clever.' He cleared his throat again. 'I knew the risk I ran, but . . .'

'But for me you thought it was a risk worth taking,' she inserted, doing her best to hold back tears that wouldn't make him feel any better if he did look at her and caught sight of them.

'I thought I stood a very good chance of the . . .' he paused, then faced the words, being the man he was, even though Devon winced to hear him end, 'of the theft not being discovered.'

She swallowed. 'But it was?' she prompted.

'Far sooner than I'd imagined,' he replied.

At his words, her mind flitted back to that first meeting with Grant Harrington. To that first time he had been in their home. 'You were hoping I would have been out of the country before you were found out?' she asked, bringing out what her intelligence had brought her.

'I had the shock of my life when I opened the door that night and saw Grant Harrington standing there,' he confessed, right there with her. 'My mind went blank for a while. I just wasn't thinking,' he recalled, 'or I would never have brought him into the sitting room where you were.'

'He came to tell you then that he knew you'd taken money from the firm?'

He shook his head. 'I'd been a bit cleverer than that,' he told her without pride. 'The—irregularities—in the finance section *had* been discovered, though they didn't point particularly to me. But the moment I saw it was Grant who had called, I knew damn well that he'd suspected it was me.' He seemed to go away from her, speaking almost to himself, as he went on, 'He could have sent anyone of half a dozen people to discuss those irregularities thrown up only because, for my sins, some immediate decision had been made to change to a more sophisticated system of paper work.'

'Why did you know that Grant Harrington suspected you when you saw him at the door?' she questioned, not wanting him to go away from her. Although he was still looking terrible, the tension that had been in him seemed to be easing.

He looked across at her then, and she tried her best to give him an encouraging smile, though in fact she was still suffering a fair degree of shock herself. The smile he offered back lifted her, weak though his smile was, as he went to answer her question.

'You wouldn't remember this, but Grant's father and I were close friends in the old days. I respected his father,' he said, and she couldn't miss the hurt in him as he paused before adding quietly, 'and he respected me,' and pressed on, 'Grant knew of this. He and I would occasionally stop for a chat. Most times his father's name would come up. I think I was a sort of link man with the man he loved very much.' He cleared his throat again, then said, 'Grant Harrington came personally that night out of the respect he had not only for me, but for his dead father. It would have been what his father would have expected him to do, much though he would hate the chore.'

Silence hung heavily when he had finished speaking. And Devon was back to remembering that night. But only then did Grant Harrington's hard look, the impolite way he had been with her, begin to mean anything. He had come there with his suspicions that her father was a thief, and she had just about confirmed it for him. He had already seen the cases in the hall, the sight of them must have given strength to his suspicions, before she had told him that she was the one who was going away, and carelessly, that she might make her stay in Stockholm that of a couple of months. He had most likely assumed that she intended to stay in only the best of hotels. Her father's salary was high, but it wasn't up to her jet-setting about the world for a couple of months, staying at only the best hotels, at any time she felt like it—and he had known that.

It seemed to her then that Grant Harrington, knowing that her father was as honest as the day was long, had not wanted to believe what the intellect behind that high forehead had told him; that through her, because of her fun-loving ways; through the love her father had for her that would deny her nothing, she had turned him into a criminal. No wonder he had been blunt with her! The great respect his father had had for her parent had been tarnished—and she was the root cause.

Her father moving to put his head in his hands brought her rapidly back to the present. She bottled down the impulse to go and put her arms around him. It would serve no purpose, though it might assure him that she still thought him the most wonderful father in the world. But she would have plenty of time to reassure him on that point, she thought, making herself stay just where she was. She knew, for all he wouldn't show it, that it would only irritate him if she went to fuss round him. More important at the moment was the need to get it all out into the open. If he was going to brood on it, then they would do it together. She had had her turn—it was his turn now.

'You said that by seeing Grant Harrington at the door, you knew it was you he was suspicious of,' she said, striving to get back to the subject that had lapsed. 'Had he any particular reason for thinking it might be you?'

'He's no fool, Devon,' she was told. 'He knew that if anyone of his staff was capable enough with figures to perpetrate an—embezzlement such as was perpetrated, there were few in that office up to my standing.'

'He came to accuse you?'

He shook his head. 'He planted the facts in front of me, and asked if I could throw any light on them.'

'You said you couldn't?'

'I—hedged. But he knew. I knew he knew, although he didn't suspend me straight away.'

'Suspend you?'

'He couldn't do anything else. He called on a Saturday night two weeks ago, to tell me not to go into the office until further notice.'

Devon had never felt so dreadful in her life. All the time she had been in Sweden, at a time when her own anguish about the success of her operation had been terrifying, her poor dear father had been facing this alone—and all because of her!

'You've given years of service to the firm,' she snatched out of thin air, unfairly not seeing Harrington's side of it in that moment of wanting to pull her father out of his despair.

'And I've been well paid for it,' he said, still loyal to the company he had robbed. And, fair where she couldn't be just then, 'And I have a lot to be grateful to Grant Harrington for.'

'Grateful—to *him*!'

'Yes, grateful. He could more easily have sent someone else to suspend me—and be justified in doing so. He could have sent any one of the senior people I work with here tonight to dismiss me and ask for my office keys.'

'Is that what he's done—dismissed you?' she asked, tears spurting to her eyes at the indignity he had had to suffer all because of her.

'He couldn't do anything else,' he said. 'The evidence against me is watertight.'

'Oh, love,' she mourned, and could no more stay put then than fly. Her high-heeled shoes had long since been dispensed with, and shoeless she went to his side, sitting on the arm of his chair and putting an arm around him as she asked, 'What's going to happen now, Dad?'

He patted the hand resting on his shoulder. 'He didn't say,' he said on a sigh. 'He just called for my keys, and told me that my suspension was over—and my job with it.'

Devon wiped her eyes with the back of her hand, glad that with his shoulders hunched before her, he could not see her tears. Oh, how much he must think of her, that he should put her before the honour he valued so much, she thought, tears threatening again.

'He—won't—prosecute, will he?' she asked, when she thought she had herself under control, bringing out the one fear that would crucify her father more than he was being crucified already.

'He'll have to,' was the flat answer she received.

'But—but his father respected you,' she brought out quickly, clutching at straws.

'There's no sentiment in business, Devon,' she was told rather severely. 'Grant has already gone farther than I could expect by calling several times in person, when he must have known after his first visit that I was as guilty as hell.'

They lapsed into silence again, Devon's mind going on to wonder if Grant Harrington would let her father off if somehow, from somewhere, they could pay the money back. But how? It ran into thousands, she knew it did. She didn't know the exact figure, but she knew that her treatment had not come cheaply. But from where could they get so much as a thousand pounds? It was hope . . .'

'The house!' she said suddenly, excitedly, as her father slewed round in his chair to see what was making her so excited. 'We could sell the house. We could give the money to Harringtons, and move into a . . .'

'The bank has first call on the house, child,' he interrupted, revealing something she had never known. And it was then that it came home to her just exactly how much of a drain she had been to him and his resources.

'It was worth it. Never think that it wasn't,' he said, reading her expression. 'You had to have the best treatment I could get for that hip of yours.' He squeezed her hand. 'You had to.' And, taking his turn to make her feel better, 'No one would ever know now that there was ever anything wrong with you.'

'You didn't tell—Grant Harrington why you needed to take some of his money? That it was so that I could have the operation?'

'The money was gone. What it was used for was immaterial,' he said. 'I broke faith with the company, and that's all that counts in business.'

As her father had said, the money had been taken, the trust broken, the rest—immaterial. But she didn't have to remember farther back than her encounter with Grant Harrington tonight, to know that he was still of his fixed opinion that she had blithely frittered away every penny of her father's income—and more. Not knowing about her operation, he had been certain, and had been right about one thing—the money had gone on her.

The elation she had been feeling when she had entered the house was gone for ever, and she was made to feel even more weepy when her father suddenly said:

'I'm sorry that your home coming had to be like this,' making her think that had she not arrived at precisely the wrong moment, he would have gone on covering up for as long as he could. 'Whatever happens, whether or not I have to go to prison,' that word 'prison' turning her blood to ice, 'it will all have been worth it.' And she thought her heart would break when, with so much on his plate, he tried for a cheery note, and said, 'Now isn't it about time I heard what's been happening to you? We'll crack the sherry open to celebrate, and you can tell me all about it.'

CHAPTER THREE

DEVON awoke the following morning with everything as fresh in her mind as it had been through her many waking hours during the night.

Without any joy in her she had entered into the façade of a happy homecoming. She had sipped a medium dry sherry with her father, and had recounted the lighter parts of her post-operative treatment.

With all that was hanging over him, she had made no mention of the occasional niggle she still felt in her hip. And she had made no mention either of Dr Henekssen's instruction that she should take frequent periods of rest. Her operation had cost her father dear. It had cost him his honour. He had said it was worth it—for his peace of mind, he had to believe that.

'The operation was one huge success,' Devon had told him, knowing it would prove true once she had had her final check over with Mr McAllen, though there were still some weeks to go yet before the consultant would put her file permanently away. 'Dr Henekssen said that I can do anything I ever wanted to do,' she had tacked on brightly, leaving out that the doctor had qualified his statement with the prefix 'In a while'.

Her father had smiled then, and she had smiled back as he had thought to question whether she would have to see her own consultant again.

'In about five weeks from now, but it's only a formality,' she said confidently. 'You know how these doctors are, they never like to let you out of their clutches.'

Devon got out of bed, her thoughts with her father and

far from happy. The only light in the darkness of the prison sentence looming over him was that she was able to walk straight away without having to wait for her hip to get the message that she wanted to be on her way.

Guilt sped in to be her companion, and stayed with her as she went downstairs. How could there be light in any of this, when because of her, her father had sacrificed the honour he held so dear?

She entered the kitchen with an impotent desire to do something, but with no idea of what it was she could do to avert her parent facing, after all he had been through, the final ignominy of serving a term in jail.

But when, her father down first, she took one look at the man who had not counted the cost to himself, to his incorruptibility, when it came to putting her first, and she saw that he was looking worse than ever this morning, so Devon knew that she could not just stand idly by while they waited to learn if his lot was to be a term in prison.

'Morning, Papa,' she said, dropping a light kiss on his grey cheek. 'You sit down with your paper, I'll see to breakfast.'

Talk in the kitchen where they always breakfasted was spasmodic. But many times as she searched for some way out of the frightening future that loomed, she caught his eyes on her and the easy way she now moved around.

It was when she joined him at the table, the thought in her mind that there was no need for him to get a move on this morning—he had no office to go to—that that word 'office' triggered off an idea in her mind.

The idea grew, began to take shape, and then became urgent enough to be acted upon. But she knew she would have to go carefully. He would oppose the idea, she knew that, even as she admitted to feeling sick inside at what she was going to do.

It was ten past nine when, taking care not to give him

the least chance for suspicion, delaying her errand by flicking a quick duster around, casually, and for the second time since she had come home, Devon was again at pains to prevent him knowing the truth of a matter.

'Dr Henekssen said I should take regular exercise,' she dropped out. 'I think I'll change into something respectable and go into town.'

She caught his quick look, and was on pins for a moment in case he had seen through her. She saw his brows knit together, and knew his brain was at work. Then suddenly he smiled an understanding smile, and without offering to go with her, he said quietly, 'You do that, love.'

Knowing him well, Devon felt relief as she hopped on to his wavelength. The understanding in his smile meant, she saw, that he had not guessed at what lay behind her reason for wanting to go into town; he thought, the dear man, that now that she had lost her feeling of wanting to hide herself away, she wanted at the first opportunity to lay the ghost of her aversion to entering any of the many stores in Marchworth town centre.

She was on her way to her room, her mind on which of the few smart clothes in her wardrobe she would wear, when he called her back.

'Before you do anything, I think it would be a good idea to make that appointment with Mr McAllen,' he said, and caused her to swallow down fresh tears, that whatever dreadful troubles he had of his own, as always he was still putting her first.

'I don't have to see him for ages yet,' she reminded him.

'Do it now, Devon,' he said firmly. 'You know from past experience that we've had to wait ages to get an appointment when we've wanted to see him in particular, and not one of his team.'

She could see it would only worry him if she didn't do it

now. But she wanted to be on her way with all speed; in her view he had got more than enough worries to be going on with. Though not for much longer if she . . .

'Fusspot,' she said lightly as she went to the phone.

'Done,' she said a few minutes later. 'Lucky, though, that I didn't want an appointment in the next couple of weeks—Mr McAllen is away on holiday.'

'The usual Thursday clinic?' he enquired to delay her when she was anxious to be away.

'Thursday is booked solid. But they managed to fit me in on the Monday session in five weeks' time,' she told him, edging to the door.

Up in her room, after spending some moments in rejecting everything except the suit she had worn yesterday, Devon surveyed herself in the wardrobe mirror. Any other garment would have been preferable, she thought, remembering all too clearly Grant Harrington's cynical eyes travelling the length of her last night. He had decided then that either he or some other man was out of pocket on account of her suit, she knew, but all the same, the smart cut of it gave her confidence that nothing else in her wardrobe would afford.

Needing all the confidence she could get, she hesitated only briefly before putting her feet into her new black shoes. Then, not allowing herself to dwell on the wisdom of wearing shoes with a heel when she had had so little practice, and trying not to dwell either on the mammoth task she had set herself, she left her bedroom and went to say cheerio to her father.

The main offices of Harrington Enterprises were housed away from the industrial area where they had a few offices and their principal factory, but the main offices were not too far from the town centre. And had she thought Grant Harrington would have agreed to see her if she telephoned for an appointment first, Devon would have stopped off at a telephone box on the way and made a call.

But without effort recalling the arrogant way he had looked at her as though she was of no account, Devon knew he would be more likely to give instructions that she should not so much as enter the building, much less his office.

And yet he was going to see her. She was determined on that, even if the palms of her hands were moist as she stood in front of the plate glass doors, her insides quaking at the thought of the short shrift she could count on receiving from him.

A picture of her father came into her mind, and she was seeing again not his proud bearing, but his hunched shoulders, his face grey, as it had been that morning. It was all she needed to have her pushing the doors inwards. And courage, born of love for him, had her going straight up to the desk and asking to see Mr Grant Harrington.

'You have an appointment.'

Devon had thought this one out while she had been getting changed. 'Naturally,' she replied, managing to look as though, like the receptionist, she thought it inconceivable that she should expect to see him without one. 'Grant did tell me where in this vast building his office is,' she confided, 'but . . .'

The young receptionist caught on, her smile warmer now that she realised that it was not a business appointment the super blonde had, but an appointment of a more personal nature.

In no time, Devon had the directions she needed, and was travelling up in a lift knowing that the rest of her quest was not going to be as easy. But she was determined that, having got this far, she would wrap herself around the legs of Grant Harrington's desk if he tried to eject her before he had heard her out.

Stepping out of the lift, she counted down the doors along the corridor, and overcoming the fact that her insides were starting to feel like jelly, she hesitated only briefly at the one she had to go through, then, too het up to think of knocking first, she opened the door and went straight in.

But she was to find that if she had been expecting to see Grant Harrington straight away, then she was in for a big disappointment. For there was only one person in the pale green airy office to which she had been directed, and that person was not him, was not even male, but a dark-haired female of about thirty-five, who looked up from the matter she was typing and showed her a professional smile of enquiry.

'I'm—I'm sorry,' Devon got out. And, pulling herself together, 'I must have got the wrong door—I was looking for Mr Harrington's office.'

'I'm Mr Harrington's secretary,' the woman replied, her professional smile still in place.

Devon found a smile of her own from somewhere. 'Oh, good,' she said bravely, 'Then Grant can't be far away.'

The professional smile stayed put, and it was then that she knew her strategy had come unstuck. The girl on reception had been younger, less up to the ruses that might be deployed to see the very busy head of the Company.

'If you'd like to take a seat, Miss . . .' She waited for a name that wasn't forthcoming, then went on, 'I'll advise Mr Harrington that you're here.'

By this time Devon's eyes were taking in her surroundings. There were three chairs nearby, placed opposite the secretary's desk, so that must be where people usually sat and waited to see him. She spotted a door to the other side of the desk, and knew then that that was where she would find the man she had screwed up all her courage to come here to see.

Well, she wasn't going to be put off at the first obstacle, she thought, aware that the secretary had lost her smile and was watching her. 'I'll . . .' Devon said, and pivoted to move quickly towards the door—too quickly in her haste. She felt a sharp pain in her right hip, and the rest of her sentence, the 'I'll advise him myself,' never got uttered.

A panic of a different kind beset her. She felt winded by the thoughts that came rushing in that her operation had not been a success! And, afraid she would topple over, as had not been unknown, she sank into the seat nearest to her. It must be because of the heels she was wearing, it must be, she thought, as the pain started to subside.

'I didn't get your name,' pressed the woman she had forgotten was there, her smile back in place now that her invitation to take a seat had been complied with.

'Er—Johnston,' said Devon, her mind more concerned with holding down her panic, with telling herself that she would be all right in a minute, that in a minute she would be fit to go through that other door.

As soon as she was sure her hip wasn't going to let her down, Devon thought, she would carry out her intention to go through that other door. The last thing she wanted was to collapse in a heap at Grant Harrington's feet. I'll go now, she thought, deriding her fears that her hip might not hold her.

But it was already too late. She had delayed too long. The secretary, after a swift flick across to note her ringless left hand, was already speaking into the intercom.

'There's a Miss Johnston here to see you, Mr Harrington. I haven't got her appointment recorded, but . . .'

'Johnston?' She'd know that voice anywhere. And, after the briefest of pauses, there was aggression, she knew too, mixed in with incredulity at her cheek, if it was who he thought it was, when the abrupt enquiry came, '*Devon* Johnston?'

The secretary looked her way for confirmation or otherwise. Dumbly, Devon nodded. She heard confirmation of her name passed from one to the other. But when perhaps she should not have been totally surprised at the message that came back, a message which he knew she would hear, what did surprise her was the spontaneous combustion his words set off, firing her pride into such instant fury that she forgot she was there to beg and plead if need be.

'Be good enough to make a note, Wanda,' he instructed curtly, 'that I have no time to spare now—*or ever*—for Miss Johnston or any of her sort.'

Fury such as Devon had never known shot to an immediate peak, her pride cut to the bone. Who the devil did he think he was, that he could belittle her so in front of a *third* person? How *dared* he!

Barely aware that the intercom had been switched off, heedless that the secretary was looking at her as though asking if she would like her to repeat the message, Devon was on her way.

Not pausing to think twice—or even think at all— smartly she left her chair and circumnavigated the desk. And while Wanda was staring incredulously after her, she was barging her way in through the door of the adjoining office, not stopping until she was face to face with the man she had come there to see.

Slowly the big tall man rose from behind his desk, the look he burned her with as he saw she had sprinted past his secretary not promising. Black brows came down, but Devon was unrepentant, and stood with her feet firmly planted on the thick-piled carpet.

Grant Harrington moved ominously from behind his desk and advanced towards her. But, when it looked as

though he would pick her up with his all male strength
and toss her back the way she had come, whether from the
indignant look of her, or whether because he didn't want
another interruption to his day if she tried barging in
again, he stopped when Wanda, who Devon was just
realising had chased after her, said, 'I'm sorry, Mr Harrington. She just took off—I couldn't . . .'

'Since she's in,' he told his secretary, 'I'll deal with her,'
which to Devon's ears sounded no more promising, and
just as insulting as his other remarks.

The door was then slammed shut as Wanda went out.
And as he came away from the door, Devon was again on
the receiving end of those dark eyes, his lips curling as
those eyes swept over her Swedish suit.

He did not invite her to sit down—she hadn't expected
him to. 'Make it short,' he rapped. 'I'm busy.'

'I . . .' she began sharply. And was then all of a sudden
all too well aware, that she was in no position to show
angry pride. She was here to ask him, to beg him if need
be, not to send her father to prison.

'Spit it out,' he barked impatiently. 'And be quick
about it!'

Devon saw again her father as he had been. It forced
down her ire, and gave a beating to her reluctance to beg
for anything from this sour-faced grey-suited man who
had no time to waste on the likes of her.

'I've come to ask you not to prosecute my father,' she
told him flatly.

And she was then forced to stand quietly by, while he
moved past her to his desk and showed her his back for
long moments. He turned abruptly, but was to pin her
with those dreadfully cold hard eyes for several seconds
more before, with a sudden unexpected mocking note, he
taunted:

'Give me just one good reason why I shouldn't.' That

mocking note told her that she could give him a hundred reasons, and that the outcome would be just the same.

'Because . . .' The moment was there when she should tell him that her father had only taken that money for her operation. But as she looked back at him, stared at the tall virile man who was such a splendid specimen of fitness and health, a man who she knew indisputably had never had a thing wrong with him in his life—so Devon saw he would never understand how desperate her father must have felt to have done such a thing.

'Well?' he prompted brusquely. Not a man to wait long for anything, she observed, as she made herself think positively, that, having got so far, she *had* to try. Soon he was going to lose patience with her altogether. Any second now she might well find herself being pushed head first out through that door she had just barged her way in through.

'Because I—don't want you to.' It had not been what she had meant to say, but with his fierce eyes pinning her, nerves were making her tongue-tied.

It did not surprise her that he looked her over with a contempt he did nothing to hide. But he did not keep her waiting very long before he poured the vitriol she had been expecting down over her head. Though what he said was short and to the point, and left her in no doubt that her plea not to prosecute her father had fallen on very stony ground.

'In my view, Miss Johnston,' he told her malevolently, 'you've had altogether too much of what *you want*.'

It was clear from that that he was determined to prosecute. 'Oh, please,' she begged, even while knowing from the set look of him, that she was pleading in vain.

'Oh, please,' was mimicked back to her. Then, his tone hardening, 'It's a bit late in the day to suddenly get round to wondering what your friends will say when they hear your father has gone to prison for stealing from his employers.'

Devon felt what colour she had leave, but she got no sympathy from the man watching her. The thought of her father in prison was making her legs feel weak, so that she would dearly have liked to have sat down.

'Please,' she said, gathering what strength she could, she had to try and get through to this iron hard man, 'please don't send him to p-prison. He didn't—didn't take the money for himself.'

'I know that, you avaricious little bitch!' was blasted at her. 'It should be you serving a jail sentence, not him!' he roared, his control on his temper going, as he continued, 'You took and took from him—a man whose integrity I would have staked my life on, so that he had to resort to stealing to keep you in the style you coveted!'

Devon could take him hurling words of wrath about her head, though strangely, the thought impinged that Grant Harrington needed his fury to rid himself of the tremendous shock he too had received to have his belief in her father's integrity shattered.

But he was gaining control of his shot temper. She heard his voice even, when, presenting her with his back once more, he went towards the door, knowing before he spoke that the interview was over.

'You've wasted enough of my time,' he said, and there was an assured finality there as he added, 'Goodbye, Miss Johnston.'

'*Stop!*'

That one sharply spoken word had him pausing. His hand left the handle of the door just as he had been going to open it for her to go through, and he moved towards her until he was only a few feet from her. And there was no mistaking the glint in his eyes that close.

'*You*,' he stated with emphasis, 'are in no position to

give orders to anybody.' He then looked ready to pick her up and put her the other side of that door if she didn't soon voluntarily move herself.

'You don't,' she got in quickly before he could lay a finger on her, 'you don't know what it was he sp-spent the money on.' She knew she was stammering, but time was closing in.

Again she was made to suffer the way his eyes swept over her Swedish suit. 'Strange as it might seem, I do not require an itemised account,' he gritted—going on to advise her, 'I'm quite able to reason by just looking at you why it is my books don't balance.' And insolently, his eyes appraising her suit again, 'Odd though you may find it, it doesn't overstretch me to guess that your wardrobe must be full to overflowing with foreign numbers similar to the one you have on.' Too late now to wish she had presented herself wearing anything other than her smart suit, as he hazarded another guess. 'And it wouldn't be tourist class for you on your trips abroad, Miss Johnston, would it? Not for you the mingling with the common masses; it would have to be first class all the way, wouldn't it?'

How long she had been closeted with him in his office, Devon had no idea. But suddenly, after she had gone through the emotions of feeling sick, of having damp hands and weak limbs, not to mention spurting pride, his blatant goading of her was making her angry again.

'The money wasn't spent on any of those things,' she flared, but was again subdued when his eyes flicked her suit. 'Well, yes, I—I bought this suit while I was in Sweden,' she said, hating him afresh. 'But I wasn't in Sweden enjoying myself.'

'Shame,' was his sarcastic offering, sending her ire soaring. 'Out of season for rich playboys, was it?'

'Damn you!' she snapped, wanting to hit his cynical face. And, riding on temper, the words were rocketing from her, 'I went to Sweden because I needed an operation!'

Her anger fell away as she saw the sharp look he gave her. And the thought crossed her mind that if nothing else, then at least she had knocked his hateful, cynical, disbelieving sarcasm on the head. Promptly she was to be proved wrong.

'Ah,' he said, and in her view, much too ready with his quick assumptions, 'Abortion, was it?' And while she was staggering from that, 'You needn't have gone to Sweden for it, surely?'

To have revealed her need for surgery to an outsider— the other operations she had had like this one being talked of to no one—and then to have him come back with that cynicism, plus more insulting remarks, was just too much.

'You—*swine*!' she hissed. And without a thought in her head that she had been ready to grovel to him, so with those words, her hand flashed to the side of his face.

'Cool it!' he thundered, and had caught her wrist in a fierce grip the moment before her hand would have connected.

She saw a light she didn't understand in his eyes as they looked into the blazing blue flame in hers. Though she hardly thought it was admiration as he threw the wrist in his grasp from him as though offended to have to touch her.

But as her fury did indeed start to cool, so she began to wonder—had that really been her who, had he not stopped her, would have given him a vicious swipe across his face? She had no time to go into this new person she had become, for he was going on, though still sarcastic, to change his opinion that it was for an abortion that she had journeyed to Sweden.

'Forgive me,' he said, not an atom of apology in his

voice, his look, or anywhere about him. 'It wasn't an abortion, was it?'

She was wary of him now, the heat in her gone. 'No, it wasn't,' she replied quietly.

'But it was an operation?'

Devon had no belief in his changed mild tone. It had her hesitating to tell him anything. 'Er—yes,' she said. 'Yes—that was the reason I went away.'

His look said he thought she was lying through her teeth. But if she was so taut that it wouldn't have surprised her had she snapped in two, then she saw, by the way he propped himself against his desk and studied her, that Grant Harrington was completely relaxed.

'Which brings us to the crunch of why you're here,' he observed, taking his study from her, to the toes of his shoes. 'What you're really saying,' he said, and paused, then looked sharply up, 'is will I not prosecute your father for robbing me,' he paused again, deliberately she felt, 'in the tragic circumstances of your needing the money for a life-saving operation.'

Her eyes had been hypnotised by his, hope in her at the start that he was beginning to have some understanding. But as he came to an end, only then did Devon realise that he was baiting her.

And again she wanted to hit him. She wanted to rant and rail at him. Wanted to verbally abuse him as he was abusing her. But she had to choke down what she was feeling. She was in no position to sling insults back at him. Her dear self-sacrificing father would go to prison if she didn't hang in there and stick it out.

'It wasn't—a life-saving operation,' she told him tonelessly.

'Plastic surgery?' One eyebrow arched. 'You were beautiful before you went,' he remarked without making it sound like a compliment. Though he surprised her with his matter-of-fact statement—because, if he thought her beautiful, then he had managed to keep that opinion well hidden. 'Have a hang-up about the shape of your bosom, did you?' he enquired mockingly. And, his eyes taking stock of her breasts, 'They did a good job,' he observed laconically.

Devon lowered her eyes from dark eyes that stripped her, but when she raised them a second later, she saw that all baiting had gone from him and that he was looking tough again, looking again ready to throw her out on her ear.

'Oh, please,' she begged, getting in while she still had a chance; before she would feel his hands on the lapels of her suit hauling her to the door. 'My father only did what he did for me. Don't—please don't send him to prison!' The dark eyes on her were impervious to her pleading, as hard and unrelenting they looked back at her. 'If—if anyone should be punished, it should be me,' she ended.

'At last we agree on something,' he replied. And, forcefully, 'Had you not been so set on careering around the world enjoying yourself, had your father thought to spank your rear end instead of giving you everything you craved from infancy, then I doubt very much he would have broken the trust I, and my father before me, placed in him.' And his anger was loosed again at that broken trust. 'The fault *is* yours, you spoilt, mercenary little parasite,' he reviled her. 'Had you not been so intent on having a good time . . .'

'I wasn't having a good time,' she butted in hotly, flaring up at his unflattering description of her. 'I was . . .' As suddenly as it had come, the heat receded, making her falter over what she was telling him. 'I've—only just—left hospital.'

That she had for the moment floundered was little more than she should expect, she thought. For so long all anger in her had lain dormant, so it was hardly surprising that having felt the stirrings of anger more since she had known him than in the last six years, this new person she had become should falter.

But he was not seeing that her floundering was a result of her emerging from her quiet passive shell. He saw, she knew he did, that her hesitating when telling him she had only just come out of hospital was further confirmation that she was trying to pull the wool over his eyes with nothing but a string of lies.

'Just when *did* you come out of hospital?' he asked, when she just knew he wasn't believing that she had ever been hospitalised.

'Er . . .' Devon was hesitating again. 'Two days ago,' she said, knowing fresh confusion as she tried to back track. 'Er—no, it wasn't,' she said, the two nights she had spent in a Swedish hotel mixing up her arithmetic. 'It was Tuesday.'

'If you're going to invent stories, Miss Johnston,' he told her coldly, 'then might I suggest you write all the facts down to check that they all tie in before you glibly trot them out.' And while she wanted to flare up again, he was coolly complimenting, 'Though I must say your powers of invention are far greater than those of your father.'

'What do—you mean?' she asked, and was soon to learn that he gave no weight to her story whatsoever, when sarcastically he replied:

'Extraordinary, wouldn't you say, that in the two or three conversations I've had with your parent since this matter came to light, never once has he pleaded mitigating circumstances?' And before she could get in, as heatedly she wanted to, 'Extraordinary, don't you think, that never once did he mention this operation it was so vital you should have?'

'He wouldn't mention it,' she retorted, anger rising at

his sneering. 'He wouldn't mention it because . . .' she could feel herself starting to get flustered, ' . . . because he knows—that is—er—he knew, that I did have a—hang-up, as you suggested.' She saw he was no nearer to believing her now than he had ever been, that he thought she was latching on to the suggestion he had given her so as to make her case more plausible. But she made herself go on despite the fact that he was discrediting every word she said. 'B-but it was a hang-up about needing surgery at all.'

'Is that a fact?' he enquired, and looked purposefully at the door, everything about him telling her that in his view he had wasted more than enough time listening to her complete and utterly phoney story.

'I'm not lying,' she said desperately, searching feverishly in her mind for some way to convince him that what she was telling him was the truth. 'Mr McAllen,' she pulled from the recesses of her mind. 'He's my consultant in England,' she said in a rush, excitement rising that he couldn't doubt Mr McAllen's word. 'He knows all about me. He can . . .' she stopped, and excitement evaporated.

'He can . . . ?' prompted Grant Harrington sourly.

'Well—if he was here,' she said lamely, 'he could tell you all about . . . Only . . .'

'Only?' he enquired with that lofty cynicism she hated.

Just as much as she hated having to tell him,' 'Only he's—away on holiday at the moment.'

'How very inconvenient!' She hated him too. 'How about if I write to your doctor in Sweden?' he suggested, 'I'm sure he won't be too busy to drop me a confirming line. Though of course he would have to write to you first for permission to give me details. But it shouldn't take more than two or three weeks for letters to go back and forth, and meantime I might have forgotten all about taking legal proceedings.'

Stunned by the sort of mind he had, Devon stared at him and saw she could have saved all the breath she had used in trying to get through to him. For as his eyes went like cold steel, Grant Harrington had only one more word to say to her, when, not bothering with politenesses, he pointed to the door.

'Out!' he said, and he meant it.

'Please,' she begged, at her wits' end. Her father had done so much for her, she just couldn't fail him. 'Please don't prosecute him,' she said hurriedly, spurting on still trying to get through. 'Prison would kill him, and—and he didn't take the money for himself—the debt is mine.'

Arrogantly he looked at her, his tone as cold as his eyes. 'So when are *you* going to repay me?'

'Repay you . . .'

'You've said the debt is yours.'

'I'll work,' she galloped in before he had barely finished, thinking she saw a chink in the brick wall of unrelenting male in front of her. 'I'll work hard—I'll work for you if . . .'

'Not if I have anything to do with it,' was his uncompromising answer, sarcasm on its way, as he took fresh and insulting stock of her, and then drawled, 'What sort of work did you have in mind? Your doctor says you're fit enough for those sort of—er—gymnastics, does he?'

For a moment Devon just wasn't with him. 'He said I would have to take care not to overstrain my . . .' she stopped, his meaning hitting her like a cold shower. She took a deep breath, her hands clenched at her sides for control. 'I meant office work,' she told him coldly.

'You know anything about office work?' How she detested everything about this man! 'Come to that,' he continued, uncaring of the wrathful look she threw him, 'do you know anything about work at all?'

All she knew was keeping house, and her liking for him

did not go up in any fashion that because he was waiting
for an answer, she was forced to confess:

'Well, not really, but . . .' Sharply she was cut off.

'What you're saying is that at no time since completing
your *formal* education have you earned money to pay your
way?'

Unspeaking, she nodded. And she saw then that his
temper was near to being on the loose again, so that it
wouldn't have surprised her if he'd hurled 'idle bitch!' at
her once more.

But he had done with words, and action was far more
effective as, taking her roughly by the arm, he pulled her
with him to the door. And Devon knew then that her quest
had failed, that any second now she would be on the other
side of that door.

'Please, Mr Harrington,' she pleaded, ignoring this
time the twinge in her hip as his smarter stride had her
breaking into a trot. 'I'll do anything for you,' she begged,
she'd scrub floors, anything, if only . . .

'Lady,' he said, looking down at her from his lofty
height, his hand already on the handle, his eyes going
disparagingly down over her, 'there's *nothing* you can offer
that I'm likely to want.'

The next thing Devon knew was that there was a closed
door between them, and that she had very firmly been
placed on one side—while he had stayed on the other.

CHAPTER FOUR

THE weekend that followed her fruitless visit to see Grant
Harrington was, Devon thought when Monday finally
arrived, the worst weekend she could remember.

Her father had gone from merely looking terrible to
looking haggard. The worst of it was that whenever he
caught her looking at him, his face would assume a cheery
expression as he tried to show that he didn't have one
single thing worrying him now that she was back minus
her limp.

The postman dropping an electricity bill through the
letter box had her shooting into the hall, small relief
coming to her build-up of tension, that a bill was all that
had been delivered. She had thought it might be a court
summons—though since she had no real idea how one
received notice that one was to be prosecuted, whether it
be by a policeman calling at the door initially, or however—she was on thorns the whole time. The only thing
she was certain of was that that disbelieving swine of a
man Grant Harrington would be prosecuting.

'Charge of the light brigade,' she told her father, the
best she could do by way of humour as she handed over
the brown envelope.

The morning dragged on, neither of them referring to
what was in the forefront of both their minds.

It was May, but the weather had turned cold. 'I've
made you your favourite streak and kidney pudding for
lunch,' Devon said, having noted that her father had eaten
as little at breakfast as she had.

'Oh, good!' he replied. But she had seen through his

57

forced enthusiasm, and didn't need the evidence of his only half cleared plate, although he had tried hard to get it down, to know that the poor love had little appetite for anything.

During the afternoon he went outside to cut the front lawn. And watching him from the sitting room window, Devon could have howled that, since he did not realise he was observed, she should see him look so wretched.

Unable to bear watching him and at the same time keep tears from falling, she turned away. And again her mind went searching and searching, as it had done ever since Grant Harrington had forcibly ejected her from his office on Friday. There *must* be something, some way, in which she could save her father from prison. There *had* to be a way!

The ringing of the telephone cut short her darting up fresh and equally futile avenues. Seldom was it that anyone telephoned; more often than not, the only calls they received were people dialling wrong numbers.

Picking up the phone, Devon answered with their number. Then, for one paralysed moment, she very nearly dropped the instrument. For the voice that greeted her, no more civil than the last time she had heard it, was oh, so clearly remembered, as was every word he had ever said to her.

'Grant Harrington,' he announced himself. And as her thoughts darted everywhere as she gripped onto the phone, he was saying shortly, 'I want to see you.'

'Me?' she exclaimed, tension, surprise, making her voice husky. Then, with hope in her heart, whether it be foolish to have hope or not after the way he had been with her, 'Yes, of course,' she said hurriedly, terrified suddenly that if his call was on account of some softening in him, then she had to agree, agree to anything before he changed his mind. 'I'll come straight away,' she rushed on, her mind already consumed with the idea of a taxi to get her to his office the quicker.

'Not now,' he barked down the wires. 'I've wasted enough of my working time on you.'

Knowing she'd take the next rocket to the moon if that was where he wanted her to meet him, her voice more controlled now she had got over her initial shock, Devon took time out only to take a grip on her nerves.

'Where? When?' she asked, hoping she wasn't going to have to wait a week.

'Come to my home. Tonight. Seven-thirty,' was briskly rapped at her.

Supremely confident, he didn't wait for any objections, which wouldn't have been forthcoming anyway, but tersely he gave her his address. And as Devon recognised where he lived as being the select end of town, he still wasn't waiting—the next thing she heard, was the dialling tone in her ear.

Only then, after he had hung up, did she have space to get her thinking into order. That she thought him bossy, arrogant and rude went without saying. And swine was too good a name for the man who knew he had her just where he wanted her. He knew, the arrogant devil, from the way she had been ready to go down on her knees to him, that she would eagerly jump to any tune he called.

But what he thought, what she thought, was of no importance. The very fact that he was willing to see her must mean, mustn't it, that he too had gone over again every word that had been said? Perhaps—she gulped at the enormity of that 'perhaps'—perhaps having gone over again all she had told him, he now *did* believe her, *did* believe she had had an operation. Oh, wouldn't it be fantastic, too wonderful, if, in the light of that—if in the light of the knowledge he had of her father's previous unswerving integrity, he was prepared to believe that there had been very real extenuating circumstances for what he had done! That maybe—just maybe—he had changed his mind about prosecuting!

The question then raised itself of why then hadn't Grant Harrington asked to speak to her father. Why then hadn't it been her father that he wanted to see at his home that night?

The answer evaded her, unless of course it had something to do with her telling him of her past hang-up; about her father keeping the information about her needing an operation to himself. Perhaps he had guessed that her father had not known about her visit to him on Friday. Maybe he was more sensitive than she had seen, and had thought her father might be distressed to learn that not only had she been to see him, but that she had told him about her operation herself.

Admitting she was growing confused, because that still did not explain why he wanted to see her and not her father, Devon gave it up. What did it matter? What was more important than anything, was that if Grant Harrington wasn't playing some diabolical game with her just for the pure hell of it, then there still had to be a chance to save her father. As far as she was concerned, she was ready to call at his house at any time, day or night, to grab at that chance with both hands.

It was over tea, hoping her father wouldn't think her a hardhearted Hannah to leave him when a spot of company might help prevent his thoughts from going around in the same tortuous circles she knew they were travelling, that she told him she was going to the cinema that night.

Charles Johnston looked at her solemnly for a long moment, then showed that he thought her far from hardhearted. A genuine smile came her way, and quietly he said, 'You do that, love.' And Devon knew then that since she had never been to the cinema on her own in her life, he thought this was just another instance of her wanting to lay old bogeys.

It was seven o'clock when she alighted from the bus that dropped her a fair distance from the house she had to present herself at. She admitted to feeling highly nervous about the outcome of the interview. But would not, could not, allow herself to think that Grant Harrington's sole purpose in telephoning was to lift her up and then drop her heavily down into despair again, as some sort of punishment for being the sponging type of female he had all too obviously seen her as.

Her hip had started to ache by the time she reached the wide tree-lined avenue where she would find one house in particular—The Limes. But an aching hip, which a week ago would have had her panic-stricken that her operation had not after all been successful, was the least of her worries as she slowed her steps and checked her watch, as she stood by the stone pillar with its etched 'The Limes'.

She was a little early, she saw, not realising she had been hurrying, her feet going along at the same nervous pace of her thoughts. Would she lose points by arriving early?

Too stewed up to hang about now she had got there, Devon used up a few more minutes walking up a wide and seemingly endless drive. Then, approaching the steps, early or not, she was too strung up to wait any longer. Her heart and stomach vying with each other for the greater agitation, she stretched her hand forward and placed a forefinger on the porcelain bell button—and waited.

Grant Harrington answered her ring at the door himself. And from the soles of her feet, Devon found what she could in some semblance of a smile for the big man, who looked relaxed where she was knotted up, and who appeared different, in casual trousers and a light sweater, from the other times she had seen him, when he had been more formally attired.

'I'm a little early, I'm afraid,' nerves had her apologising when she saw his eyes going over her Swedish suit—decided upon after a great deal of thought, it being the smartest thing she had. Without saying a word he stood back, and Devon crossed his threshold.

'I hardly expected you to be late,' he said smoothly, as he closed the door, making her heart sink as her smile departed. She hoped the rest of the interview wasn't going to be interspersed with sarcasm.

Seeing she had no answer to make, he indicated that she should follow him as he strode over the hall and stood back to allow her to go before him into a huge, thickly carpeted sitting room, where a couple of easy chairs and a massive settee had been drawn up before a crackling log fire.

'It's—er—cold for this time of the year, isn't it?' she managed for starters, her eyes fixed on the flames in the fire.

'Take a seat,' he replied, and waited until she had perched herself on the edge of the settee before he took the easy chair to the left of her, his long legs pushed out before him.

With him looking so relaxed, Devon tried to hide her nervousness by sitting father back in the settee. From the way he had not answered her remark about the weather, she knew he wasn't interested in pleasantries either. She was here for one thing only, and the sooner she discovered if her dearest wish was to come true, the sooner she would like it.

'You asked me to call and see you,' she said, since he was at ease in his chair and was saying nothing, but seemed content with the study he was making of her clear features, from her smooth unlined forehead, her eyebrows that were naturally wing-shaped and a shade darker than her short wavy blonde hair, past her eyes to her dainty nose and shapely mouth, and on to her chin that was just this side of having a stubborn look to it.

'I was right to think you beautiful,' he replied.

Which, since it wasn't an answer at all, had her eyes going wide as the thought hit—had he been studying her just now to refresh his memory of what she looked like? Had he thought her beautiful as he had said before, but had wanted to see her again to check that his eyesight was all that it should be?

She pulled herself together, realising that since it didn't look as though he was in any hurry to get on with the interview, then she must hurry him if she could. Because otherwise she would start getting crazy panicky thoughts, that the only reason he had ordered her there was so that he could again look at what he had decided was her beauty.

'My father . . .' she began, and wondered, as the words came out huskily, if she was ever going to lose that choked note in her voice when speaking to this man.

'Ah yes,' he said. But he still seemed in no hurry, as deliberately his eyes took in the beauty of her perfect mouth, its shape slightly emphasised by the touch of lipstick she had put on to help bolster what little confidence she had.

'He—looks terrible,' she thought to mention—and knew it was the wrong thing to have said, when a hard light came to Grant Harrington's eyes, and he said:

'The reverse can be said of you.'

Obviously the sleepless nights she had spent were, by some miracle, not showing. But she didn't want the discussion to be about her.

'He's very—upset,' she tried again to bring the conversation back.

'That makes two of us,' he admitted harshly.

'I'm—sorry.'

'How sorry, I wonder?'

Her eyes went to him. Truly she couldn't have said her sympathies were at all with how Grant Harrington was feeling, and perhaps that showed in her eyes as she looked at him. For suddenly his relaxed manner had left him, and the interview she had wanted to begin some minutes before was, all at once, under way.

'You told me on Friday that you were prepared to do anything to save your father,' he reminded her, when she needed no reminding. She had said that, and she had meant it. 'Does that still hold?'

Hope wouldn't be held down. 'Of course it does,' she replied quickly. And, with that hope in her spiralling, 'I'll do anything, Mr Harrington,' she said eagerly. 'Anything. Just name it.'

She would have gone rattling on then about not having very much experience of anything but housework, but that at school she had been top of her year, and that she was more than willing to learn, when he said:

'For a start, you can call me Grant.' And when that put everything out of her mind for a second, he was reminding her of why she was so anxious to agree to anything, by smiling a mocking smile, and adding, 'Your father does.'

'Yes, of course,' she said, and managed a smile as she swallowed and reiterated, 'I'll do anything—Grant.'

'Good,' he said. But that mocking smile was still there, and he took his time before slowly he drawled, 'How soon can you move in?'

Her brow wrinkled. 'Move—in?'

Perhaps the authorities had been wrong to mark her top of her year; or her education finishing early had dulled her brain, she thought. His question had thrown her. That was until all sign of mockery left him, and he laid it concisely on the line.

'I'm asking you to come and live with me,' he announced coolly.

Devon did not mean to be deliberately obtuse. But because he had previously left her in no doubt as to the way in which he regarded her, there was not an atom of shock in her as what he had said somehow got mixed up with the memory of him answering his own front door.

'As—your housekeeper, do you mean?' she asked, thinking that since she ran her father's home without too much trouble, given that Grant Harrington's home was vast by comparison, it shouldn't be too tough a task—and that even if it wasn't a job she wanted—well, she was still prepared, as she said, eager too, to do anything.

The slow shaking of that dark head from side to side showed her she had got it wrong. 'I have a perfectly adequate daily from Monday to Friday,' he told her, keeping his eyes on her. She had not reacted at all to his asking her to come and live with him. 'Besides which,' he went on when she had gone on to think he must mean that he wanted her to clear up for him on Saturdays and Sundays, 'I just don't see you as filling *that* particular sort of role.'

Then what particular sort of a role did he mean? she had to wonder, as she refused to get annoyed at his barely veiled hint that she wouldn't know one end of a broom from the other. Then suddenly it clicked. She had been looking away from him, but as it registered—despite all the evidence to the contrary—what it was he could only mean, so her eyes shot to his. And the words were out before she could stop them, his reaction to her words even more appalled than her shocked:

'You mean—you mean you want to *marry* me!' she cried, her exclamation revealing two things; that not only did the idea of marrying him leave her horror-struck, but that she would not consider marriage to anyone.

'*Marry you*?' he exclaimed in return, looking as appalled as she had sounded. 'Ye gods!' he said, and not bothering to dress it up, 'I'm paying through the nose now without lumbering myself with you permanently!'

And while that unflattering remark went a long way to bring her out of her shock, with a shrewdness that said he had been watching and listening with closer attention than she had thought, he was asking:

'Aside from marriage between the two of us being something neither of us could stomach—what have you got against the wedded state?'

'I've—nothing—against it,' Devon denied haltingly. 'But . . .' She broke off.

Before her operation she had known that she would never marry. But since her operation, during the long hospital hours when all manner of subjects had gone through her mind, she had come to the happy conclusion that if she did fall in love, and if someone did love her enough to want to marry her, then she would marry. But that had been qualified as having to wait until after she had had the final all-clear on her hip. For should she regress, then no way . . .

'But?' Grant prompted, breaking into her thoughts, his brows drawing together at the time she was taking in giving him his answer. 'Your powers of invention are usually quicker than this—don't tell me you're slipping!'

'If you must know . . .' she began to come back snappily. Then all at once, like a bolt from the blue, it suddenly hit her what it was he had meant. Blaming her sheltered life that she had been so slow off the mark, she felt her face go a scalding red as she left what she had been saying— her thoughts staying with the incredible notion that by his swift rejection of any idea of marriage, then by saying,

'I'm asking you to come and live with me,' he must mean . . . !

'You don't usually go scarlet when you're inventing a whopper,' he sliced through her staggering thoughts. 'I can hardly wait to hear this one,' he continued hatefully. 'Don't keep me in suspense. Spit it out, Devon, and tell me about the big "but" you have against marriage.'

His reminding her of what they had been discussing had her trying to overcome her staggering thoughts. 'I—er—that is—' she began again, but she was drowning. Surely she had got it wrong? 'F-for myself—I wouldn't dream of marrying until . . .' she said, her stomach churning as other subject matter stormed her brain.

'Don't stop there. Until what?' he asked, mockery there again at the lie he was sure she was ready with.

'Until I've received the . . .' He *couldn't* be meaning what she thought he was meaning! He didn't even *like* her! '. . . the—er—final all-clear from my medical consultant.'

The harsh bark of his laugh that greeted her as she finished speaking told her he still wasn't believing she had ever felt a surgeon's knife.

'Oh, my God,' he groaned, 'spare me the gory details— I assume you *were* going to regale me with such delightful little snippets as the number of stitches you had?'

He did not wait for any reply she would have made. But he was short and to the point, leaving her knowing that, God help her, she had *not* got it wrong. That she had been right when she had thought what she had. And he was sounding angry with her too, that from his view she was showing she was a compulsive liar, as he snarled:

'Since we're doing away with marriage, there'll be no need for you to wait for your consultant to return from his *holiday* before you give me your answer.' And just in case she had forgotten his question, he gave her the two alternatives, by adding relentlessly, 'Does your father go to prison—or do you come to live with me?'

She knew now what he meant, but that hint of stubbornness her chin denoted had her hanging on still in the hope that she had misunderstood him.

'As your—wife—without marriage?' she made herself ask—and earned herself more of his loathsome sarcasm for her trouble.

'There,' he replied, enjoying himself hugely she thought, 'I just *knew* you were as bright as you look!'

Devon's first reaction, as her heart dropped to the bottom of her boots to hear that she hadn't been so dim after all, was to think no, no, no, she couldn't do it! But even as she was thinking, God, how could this cynical swine of a man expect her to go to bed with him; that part of her that would do anything to save her father made her stay where she was on the settee when all instincts would have had her leaping from it and haring out of his house.

Somehow, a tight control came that made her turn a deaf ear to that voice in her head that said she could not possibly contemplate doing what was being asked of her. She gripped firmly at that control and hung grimly on, as, her voice gone cold, she asked:

'How long—would it be for?' The tight rein she was holding threatened to slip as she saw the way his eyes moved deliberately over her as he considered his answer. And quickly, she was saying, 'Might I assume—with you not wanting to be *lumbered* with me permanently, that my—residence—here will be for a set period?'

His eyes moved to her face, but she didn't want him looking at her face either. She knew she was a tangled mass inside, but with his ghastly proposition hanging starkly in the air, she just had to know, also, that though he might detest her, there had to be something in her face—in her figure—that had stirred him to desire her.

Oh, dear God, she couldn't do it, she thought when, unspeaking, relaxed where he sat, Grant Harrington was in no hurry to answer her question. The silence lengthened, fracturing her nerves, so that it was she who broke it, conversely, sorely needing to know what sort of a sentence she was letting herself in for.

'I mean,' she choked huskily, 'how long,' she stumbled to get the words out, 'how long does it usually take before you tire of your—women?'

The mockery in his look told her he thought the halting, husky way she had spoken was just so much play-acting. 'A week,' he replied casually, giving her hope that she would only have to stick it out that long. 'A month sometimes,' he added to torment her, knowing she thought, hating him, that if he had said a year, she just wasn't in any position to object. 'Though,' he drawled softly, not missing, she was sure, the spears of hate in her eyes as she waited for him to continue, 'since you'll be the first one I've had living under my roof, it might not take that long.'

That any man could in one breath so disparagingly intimate that once he had possessed her his desire for her would soon wane; that he wouldn't want her any more; had the anger she had been too stunned to feel suddenly rearing its head. She was no man's toy, no man's plaything. She wouldn't do it!

Anger dipped as the position her father was in spiked her. But with the memory of her father, memory of how regardless of what this vile man was ready to do to him if she didn't go along with his awful plan, her father had insisted that Grant Harrington had been more than fair to him, so her anger peaked again.

'My father *respected* you,' she threw at him hotly, all the loathing she was capable of injected into those four words.

But only, like lightning, to have Grant Harrington out

of his chair, his anger instantly loosed—more at her words than at her tone, she thought, as threateningly he stood over her, and roared furiously:

'And I bloody well respected him!' And his voice cutting as it quietened and he turned to stare into the log fire, he told her, 'There wasn't a man in my employ I respected more for his integrity than Charles Johnston.'

He moved then, from the fire, from her, and went over to a drinks cabinet. An unapproachable look was on his face as she watched him take out a bottle of Scotch and pour himself a measure. She saw he looked fed up suddenly, and all at once while some sixth sense was telling her that the unfeeling man she had thought him had somehow been deeply hurt by what her father had done, she was suddenly afraid, because of that deep hurt, that he was going to change his mind!

Even while the price he had asked of her for her father's freedom was a price she did not want to pay, she was suddenly terrified that he was re-thinking, and that he was deciding that the possession of her was not a very good exchange for not only the loss of thousands of pounds, but his shattered faith in a man he had been sure he could trust above all others.

'Grant—' she began on a choky cough, getting to her feet, needing to get in quickly to tell him that she would do all he asked.

Her speaking his name had him looking at her over the rim of the crystal in his hand. And she had a terrible feeling then, from the granite look in his eyes, from the dreadful harsh look of him, that if she said so much as one word about being ready to accept whatever terms he proposed, she could lose her father every chance of escaping prison.

'You know the way out,' he confirmed curtly, his voice arctic.

Dark despair was all hers again. She was afraid to speak, afraid from the shuttered look of him that already she had lost the only chance she and her father had. And yet she couldn't just leave—as Grant Harrington wanted her to.

He took a swig from his glass, and then he was looking at her, intelligence in the proud arrogant stance of him, so that she knew he was quite well aware of why it was she hadn't moved.

Arrogance in him was the chief characteristic she noted, as he turned his back on her to pour himself another measure. 'Ring me by Friday,' he threw over his shoulder.

The bottle in his hand went down with a thud. And it was then that Devon knew, even while she wanted to stay and get it all settled now, that by the time Grant Harrington turned, he wanted her to be gone. Without another word, she left him.

CHAPTER FIVE

THAT her father's sleeping pattern was worse than hers, and she had slept only fitfully the night before, was apparent the next morning. And that he looked even more haggard than he had yesterday when Devon had joined him at breakfast told her that Grant Harrington was not going to have to wait until Friday to hear from her.

Her panicky thoughts were back when she recalled how he had frozen on her, his mood changed after she had brought up her father's respect for him. He had dissociated himself from her then, and she had thought that he had grown weary of her before she had so much as spent one night under his roof. But his 'Ring me by Friday' had to mean that he was giving her until then to decide if she was going to live with him, or if he should call in his legal people—didn't it?

That a different kind of panic would swamp her if she allowed herself to dwell on what was going to happen to her once she was installed in his house, she just did not dare to allow. Again and again she made herself think only of her dear father—she just could not afford to think of herself. More importantly, she was faced with the big 'if'. *If* she was installed into Grant Harrington's house.

'You went to bed more or less straight away when you came in last night,' said her father as he dried up the breakfast things as she washed them. 'You didn't give me a chance to ask what the film was like.'

For his sake Devon had to lie, and keep up the pretence that she had been to the cinema. He would go into heart failure if she told him where she had been—and *anything* of what had been said!

'I've—seen better films on TV,' she said.

Lying to him did not come all that easy, and it was a moment or two before she could turn her head to smile at him. There were bags appearing beneath his eyes, she noted, her heart breaking to see he looked greyer than ever this morning. He can't go on like this, she thought, it's killing him. It was killing her to have to stand by and watch him.

His announcing just then that he thought he would go and change his library books was the heavensent opportunity she needed. The time it usually took him to select fresh books should give her just sufficient time for what she wanted to do.

'If you want to be back in time for lunch,' she said with an attempt to tease, but more because the sooner he went the sooner she could get started, 'then it wouldn't be a bad idea to go now.'

'I do tend to lose all sense of time when I get there, don't I?' he agreed, managing to raise a smile at her teasing.

Half an hour later, watching from the sitting room window, Devon saw him go down the street. The moment he had turned the corner out of sight saw her with nervous fingers dialling the number of the firm he had been employed by for the last twenty-five years, up until recently.

Getting through to Grant Harrington's secretary was the easy part. Revealing her name, colour tinging her cheeks that the efficient secretary would not have forgotten the instruction that her boss did not have time to spare for Devon Johnston or any of her sort, proved more difficult.

'I assure you Mr Harrington is expecting me to call,'

she insisted when she had been firmly told that any message she cared to leave would be passed on.

She was left hanging in mid-air while she suspected Wanda counted up to twenty, and would then come back to tell her that Mr Harrington did not want to speak to her.

'Yes?' rapped a sharp voice she wasn't ready for.

'Oh—er—Hello, Mr Har—er—Grant,' she said, struggling for words, struggling for tact. 'It's—Devon John . . .'

'I *know* that.'

Trying to banish pictures of the fun time she was letting herself in for if she was allowed to live with such a grumpy brute, Devon hurried in with her request before he got fed up with waiting for her to speak and hung up on her.

'Can I come and see you?' she asked in a rush.

'I'm busy,' was the terse reply. Followed by, 'There's only one word I want from you. You don't have to see me to give me a "Yes" or "No".'

Half of her went soaring. By the sound of it—for all he had but definitely got out of bed the wrong side—it was still on! That word 'bed' had the other half of her feeling sick inside at the enormity of what she was going to have to do.

'I—wanted to—ask you something,' she said quickly, on tenterhooks lest she blew it, knowing she just wasn't in any position to put conditions, but the memory of her father's grey face forcing her on. 'It is very important.'

The pause, the silence that followed, had her holding her breath. She guessed he was thinking the same as she was—that any conditions laid down were his prerogative. Then his voice, no more charming than it had been before, was there in her ear again.

'I have a meeting in half an hour—I'll come round.'

That he hadn't waited to say goodbye before slamming

the phone down was a courtesy she should not have
expected, she thought. And that he wanted neither of the
Johnstons to soil his plush office carpeting with their
dishonest feet was no more than she should have expected.
But did his, 'I'll come round,' never dreamt of, mean
that he meant *now*? That regardless of whether her father
was in—for Grant had not deigned to enquire—
he was already on his way to discuss his awful proposition!

That his respect for her father was lower than low
helped Devon with the crushing weight of nerves and
agitation, when not many minutes later, a sleek car was
pulled up outside the house.

Since Grant Harrington's working time appeared so
valuable, she was at the front door opening it as he walked
briskly up the garden path.

'Come in,' she invited, unnecessarily, as he didn't alter
his pace but brushed past her. 'The sitting room, I think,'
she murmured, as in the hallway, the front door closed, he
turned back to look at her in her faded jeans and T-shirt—
there just hadn't been time to change into anything more
alluring, even supposing she had any item in her wardrobe that had been designed to arouse a man's interest—
vital at this stage, she thought.

Once inside the sitting room, she did not invite him to
sit; there was a sort of barely restrained energy about the
man, and she rather thought he would have refused
anyway. But she was hopeful that this would not take too
long.

'I told you last night that my father looks terrible,' she
said, trying to earn a few points by not hanging about.
'What I wanted to ask you, to discuss with you,' she
amended, aware of her precarious position, 'is the—er—
possibility of you telling him that you don't intend to
prosecute.'

He wasn't slow. 'You're saying that if I put your father out of his misery today, that your answer is yes?'

'I love my father,' she replied, and could have hit him when he offered a sarcastic:

'My heart bleeds.'

But what she wanted to do, and what she *had* to do, were two entirely opposite things. 'Will you ring him tonight?' she asked, keeping her voice as level as she could, trying to keep her face expressionless as she looked at him across the few feet of not so plush carpeting that separated them.

His reply was not immediate, and she felt her nerves begin to jangle again as his eyes flicked over her; seeing again that light she had seen in his office once before which she had discounted as admiring as, softly, he instructed:

'Come here.' And when she just looked, not having any idea why she should go closer when there could be nothing wrong with his eyesight since he appeared satisfied with what he could see of her, he tacked on idly, 'For the fee I'm paying, I'd prefer to sample the goods before I commit myself to a promise like that.'

Apparently she was not quick enough to obey him—for long arms had come out and were gripping her upper arms. The feel of his body close to hers, as with one flex of powerful muscle he had jerked her until she had moved those few feet he demanded, had two kinds of alarm shooting through her. For as his face came nearer, not only was his intention to kiss her obvious, in itself sufficient to have her fighting the instinct that would have had her pushing him away. But the sudden jolt to her hip as firm hands on her arms pulled her off her feet towards him had caused a spasm of pain to sear her.

Her numbed reaction when his mouth met hers in a seeking, mobile kiss was a non-reaction as fear rocketed through her momentarily that her operation had not been the success it just had to be. She couldn't regress to the way she had been before Dr Henekssen had performed that miracle of surgery on her—she just couldn't!

Grant Harrington pushed her away, the look on his face cold and chilling as darkly he threatened, 'We may as well forget it now, if you're not going to co-operate better than that,' made Devon promptly forget all fears real or imaginary about the success of her operation.

'I will co-operate,' she rushed to tell him quickly, the feel of his lips still imprinted on hers. But she dared not let herself dwell on that either. 'I'm—s-sorry about—just now,' she said in another rush. Then more slowly. 'It's just that—that I've got a lot on my mind at the moment.' His kiss had unnerved her, there was no saying it hadn't—and she had had only a small part of her attention on it—oh God! 'I was . . .'

Grant, his voice still threatening, had her giving him her undivided attention, as he chopped through any further excuses she would have made, deciding for himself, she heard, how he thought she was about to explain the fact that she had been wooden in his arms. And he was angry with it, she was soon to realise.

'If you so much as breathe one word of that fictitious surgery story,' he told her fiercely, 'then count on it, I'll make you eat your lies if I have to ram each one back down your throat!'

His pure aggression more than anything told her that Grant Harrington was unused to his kisses leaving a woman cold. Acknowledging for the first time that he did have a certain something, that he might have other women panting for his kisses, though assuredly not her, Devon was quick to tell him:

'I've given up on that—that story,' vowing there and then that not another word would she tell him about her need for surgery. And adding something that was giving her a very worrying time, she brought that out as an excuse for her non-co-operation. 'It's just that—I'm exceedingly anxious about what to tell my father. I—I haven't any idea what I'm going to tell him, when I leave to come to . . .'

'What do you usually tell him when you leave on similar expeditions?' His sarcasm was back, but she thought it an improvement on his blatant aggressiveness.

'I—I'll think of something,' she replied, anxious to get back to her request that her father should be advised that he did not have to face charges of embezzlement.

'I'm sure you will,' he said, not doubting it.

'And you'll . . .' she hesitated, then rephrased it, 'Will you ring him?' Hate was renewed in her that he made her wait long, long breath-held seconds, before he nodded, then said:

'I'll contact him.'

Her agitation not quieted yet, she had one more question to ask. 'Could I ask you not to—not to tell him— about what we've agreed?'

A loftily raised eyebrow told her she wasn't going to like what was coming. 'He still believes you're as innocent as your big baby blue eyes would suggest?' he asked, and it was evident that he didn't believe in her look of innocence for a moment. It irritated her, when she knew she couldn't afford to let him provoke her.

'Don't all fathers think their daughters perfect?' she heard herself retort sharply.

But she was to have the answer she wanted, as he flicked a glance to his watch and moved to the door. 'Far be it from me to shatter *his* illusions,' he barked. And he had gone.

But he did not telephone her father. For the rest of the day, after Charles Johnston returned from the library, and both of them attempted to eat something of the lunch she had prepared, Devon was jumpy for the sound of the phone. Endlessly the day dragged on. He had given his word he would phone, she thought, when teatime came and went and the phone had stayed silent.

She went over again her lack of response when he had kissed her. She should have been awake to what she should do and not what she wanted to do. That sharp pain in her hip had thrown her, she admitted. Just as she admitted, having been free of pain ever since, that she was still too much in fear of something having gone wrong with her hip, when she knew very well she had nothing to worry about on that score.

Tea was over and done with, and she was thinking of starting on dinner, when she recalled again the 'his illusions' Grant Harrington had barked at her. She had suspected before a hurt in him that her father had cheated him, and 'his illusions' served to underline that the comfortable illusions Grant had held about her father's integrity had been violently shattered, his faith broken—no wonder he didn't believe her!

A ringing at the door bell when dinner, for all she had tried to make it as appetising as possible, had gone for the main part uneaten by both of them, alerted Devon to the fact that, with their lack of visitors, it might be Grant!

'I'll get it,' said her father from habit. And since he was half way to the door, Devon had to let him.

But she was too keyed up by that time to wait passively in the sitting room for him to come back to tell her it was only someone with a charity envelope. And she was out in the hall too, by the time he had the front door open and was exclaiming:

'Grant!'

She was by now more than familiar with the sick feeling in the pit of her stomach. But she made her face composed as she heard him being invited in. Though she could do nothing about the beseeching look in her eyes when the tall figure of Grant Harrington entered the hall, and he flicked a glance at her, then addressed her father.

'I'd like a private word with you, Charles, if it's convenient.'

Having thought she knew all about anxiety, and then some, Devon ran through a gamut of emotions in the age it took for Grant to have his private word.

Desperately she wanted to know what was being said in the dining room where her father had taken Grant. It even crossed her mind to go in with a tray of coffee, to interrupt so that she could judge from their faces how the conversation was going. With difficulty she quelled the impulse.

Her father would not breathe a word to Grant about her operation, she knew that for a fact. Just as she knew things had gone too far for Grant at this stage to ask him if there were any mitigating circumstances for doing what he had. In all probability, that question had most likely been put before and her father had stayed mum.

More minutes dragged by, with Devon becoming more and more worked up, knowing that while she could guarantee what her father would not say, she had to sweat it out in fear of what Grant *would* say.

When finally that dining room door did open, there was not a cat in hell's chance that Devon would be sitting composedly in the sitting room. She was out in the hall, her quick ears having picked up the sound. And one look at her father's face was all she needed to know that Grant Harrington had not let her down!

That her father had in thirty minutes shed an unbearable burden caused her nothing but happiness. Anxiety instantly left her to see that look of joy in the eyes that sought her out. Such joy and pleasure were there that she just had to know that, whatever Grant had told him, her name had not come into it.

'I'll see Mr Harrington out, Dad,' she said, as both men started to walk towards her.

Charles Johnston hesitated. Then he beamed a smile at her, and she guessed he was again thinking of the many bogeys she had nursed in the past, one of them being that, not liking that strangers should see her walk, never had she shown anyone to the door before.

'I'll leave you to it,' he said, his beam of a smile still there as he shook hands with Grant before disappearing into the sitting room.

The joy in her father transmitted to her, Devon was not even thinking of the price she was going to be made to pay for putting that joy there as she pulled back the front door, words of heartfelt thanks hovering somewhere near the surface. But it was Grant who spoke first.

'Have you managed yet to come up with a reason to explain your absence from home?' he enquired, a silky edge there.

'Er—no,' she replied, coming rapidly down to earth— only to go sailing skywards again, when, his voice silky still, Grant mystified her by saying:

'I think you'll find an excuse won't be necessary.'

Again Devon found herself slow off the mark. But then the only thing he could be meaning presented itself to her. And suddenly she was beaming a smile at him that was very similar to the smile her father had sent her way.

'Oh, thank you, Grant,' she said, her lips curving into a beautiful smile, her eyes alight with joy and gratitude.

'You can say "thank you" more warmly than that, can't you?' he said, his voice holding a hint of mockery, but his eyes fixed on the animated look of her.

Devon rather thought she moved first. But when Grant's arms closed around her and she raised her face to kiss him, she knew that this was what he had meant. And there was no need then for him to complain about her lack of co-operation. For willingly, if inexpertly, she kissed him, finding she rather liked the way his mouth gently teased her lips apart.

She was quite breathless when at last he let her go. But she was ready to say thank you again. For to her mind, his, 'I think you'll find an excuse won't be necessary,' could only mean one thing—that Grant Harrington had not only let her father off the hook, but that clearly he had reconsidered, and was cancelling the debt completely— what he was telling her was that she had no need to go to live with him.

'That,' said Grant, his arms falling away, one hand going into his trousers pocket, 'was a decided improvement.' Still Devon smiled. 'Though I'm sure you'll be able to do better.'

Her smile started to dip.

'I—er . . .' she said, with a feeling of being a non-swimmer thrown in at the deep end, 'I'm—er—not sure . . .' It couldn't be his kiss that had clouded her thinking, she thought, floundering in confusion, as heady as his kiss had been. 'You don't mean . . .' she began, starting to see she had made a monumental mistake somewhere, when that arrogant expression appeared on his face as he rocked back on his heels as he waited for her to get it together. 'I thought,' she said, her voice gone husky again as it always did whenever emotion got to her, 'that you were meaning that—that—the deal we made was—was void.' He made no move to help her out. 'That,' she struggled, 'I wouldn't have to come to—to live with you.'

It was his turn to smile, and she didn't like it. For there was no sincerity in his smile as his hand came out of his pocket, and he held out a door key.

'*That* philanthropic,' he told her charmingly, 'I ain't.' And he was short and to the point then, as he went on to issue his instructions. 'Business calls me away for a few days, which should,' he told her bluntly, 'give you ample time to pack.' And while she just stood staring, not believing it, he was ordering, 'I shall return on Friday—be there!'

'Be there?' she echoed—and heard he had one last thing to say to her before he departed.

'You go back on your word to me, Devon Johnston, and I shall feel no compunction in going back on what I've just told your father.'

Slowly Devon returned to where her father was waiting, two glasses of sherry already poured. 'This calls for a celebration,' he said, and looked so happy, she just had to rise over her trauma. This was Tuesday—she was in fear and trembling for what Friday would bring!

As it turned out, the days before she had to go with her cases to that élite end of town to stay for what she hoped would be a minimum amount of time were so completely filled that she had little time to dwell on the fate she was committed to. For what her father had to tell her of his conversation with Grant Harrington left her gasping at the ingenuity of the man, and made clear his remark which she had so idiotically misunderstood.

For a start her father had explained that Grant had been giving serious thought to prosecuting him, but had then been swayed against that course when thinking of his years of loyal service to the firm, plus what his father would have thought of him prosecuting his old friend. He had realised he could just not do it. For her father's sake, she had smiled at him as she thought, not much he couldn't!

But, jubilantly, he had gone on to tell her that while Grant had stated that he needed to think further on the advisability of giving him his old job back—there was a job he could do for him, which would mean he was still on the payroll should anyone get the notion that he had left the firm under a cloud.

Naturally her father had grabbed at the chance—and had then been told of a feasibility study Grant wanted carrying out in a remote part of Scotland, the idea being that after costing and so forth had been completed, consideration be given to setting up a plant there. Grant had apparently thought of him for the job because of his brilliance with figures.

'It's all top secret, of course,' Charles Johnston said, and Devon had to smile again when he beamed at her, because it was so good to see him happy again. Even if she knew, where he didn't, just why it was so 'top secret'. She knew that whatever figures her father came up with, and he would do his job well, Grant Harrington would not be opening up a plant in the remote township of Invercardine.

Her father then went on about what he would have to take with him, and it impinged on her that she would have a bit of sorting out to do with regard to warmer clothes for him. But even as she listened to all he was saying, part of her mind was preoccupied with the thought, why was Grant Harrington bothering to get him out of the way?

She could see now that it all tied in with her going to live with him. That was why he had said she wouldn't need an excuse—he had made sure she wouldn't need one, as he had said. But why would he bother? It couldn't have anything to do with her telling him her father had respected him—he had shot round to see her this morning uncaring whether or not her father had been at home. And it couldn't by any stretch of the imagination be because he had seen she was having trouble trying to think up some good reason to give for why she was leaving, bearing in mind that living in the same town her father might get to hear that she was not a million miles away. Grant Harrington was sure her powers of invention were masterly anyway—she had his belief that she had invented an operation to show her that.

Realising her father had just finished speaking, asking her if she would have time to rinse through his favourite sweater, one which he seldom had off his back, but one which he considered might be due a birthday in the circumstances, Devon left trying to fathom Grant Harrington's motives, and replied yes, of course, before seeking confirmation that all was as she suspected, by asking:

'How long will you be away? Did Mr Harrington say?'

'Grant reckons the job should be over and done with in a month.' Devious swine, she thought, all the confirmation she could want in that reply. 'It was on the tip of my tongue to ask if you could come with me,' he continued, making her wonder as she smiled bravely how on earth Grant would have refused such a request. Though on the evidence so far, it would have presented nothing of a problem to him. 'Only he mentioned then a possibility of my needing to stay longer, and with your final,' he smiled, 'and most important visit to Mr McAllen coming up, I decided against asking him.'

'You didn't mention my appointment with Mr McAllen?' she asked quickly, and saw his look become reassuring, as he replied:

'What do you take me for?'

She smiled again because it was important that he didn't suspect all was far from right with her world. And she listened as he told her how hard he was going to work, so that if at all possible, he would be back to go with her to keep that appointment.

He had been to every other appointment with her, it seemed only right that he should accompany her on this last one when, for a change, what Mr McAllen had to say could only be good. All that he had done for her rose up in her then, so that she was having her work cut out to check tears. And nothing seemed too much to do for him in that moment. For some minutes more she let him talk on, to enjoy the tremendous relief that was his. But at the end of those minutes, Devon had only one question left to ask him.

'If I have to start sorting out your warmer clothes, you'd better give me some idea when you have to be ready.'

'I'm to start out on Friday morning,' he replied—and she wasn't surprised. 'Though lord knows when I'll get there. By the sound of it, it's somewhere out in the wilds.'

When her father's train pulled out of the station on Friday morning, and Devon had assured him she would be fine on her own, she could not help but rejoice that her last sight of him was to see how, since Tuesday, those bags had disappeared from under his eyes.

But mutiny had entered her heart when she let herself back into her home, and she went straight to pack the things she would need to take with her. She knew it was a futile mutiny, just as she knew with an honesty—given his one lapse—she had inherited from her father, that she wouldn't run away from keeping her side of that terrible bargain Grant Harrington had forced her to make.

And anyway, she thought as she slammed the lid down hard on the second of the two cases she was taking with her, how could she run away even had she been so minded? She didn't need to think back further than that threatened, 'You go back on your word to me and I shall have no compunction in going back on what I have just told your father,' to know she wouldn't be packing any running shoes.

Swine, she thought, damning him and his clever brain, not thinking to be grateful for the easy way he had got her father out of the way. Harrington's, she didn't doubt, had experts they employed to do the type of feasibility study he had sent her father on.

It was after lunch when, thinking she could delay no longer, Devon checked to see she had the key Grant had given her, and set off with her cases with about as much enthusiasm as a cat viewed a water well.

That there wasn't a taxi to be had, and that she had to make her journey by bus and struggle the final a quarter of a mile with her cases, seemed a further sign that the fates were frowning darkly on her.

She felt exhausted when she reached The Limes, and chose to set her cases down while she rang the bell. That no one came to let her in was much as she expected, but as she used her key, it felt eerie going into the house, only one room of which was familiar to her.

A stubbornness in her made her ignore her feeling of exhaustion. That same stubbornness made her turn her back on the sitting room. With a set look on her face, she trundled her cases upstairs, a determination in her not to think, as she investigated several of the bedrooms.

The room that was obviously *his* was large, high-ceilinged, and housed the largest double bed she had ever seen! Still trying to shut out thought, she backed out of that room and concentrated her mind on the thought that, the size he was, he would need a huge bed, but that she wasn't going to sleep—*sleep* in it with him.

The room next to his, close enough, she thought, if not too close, but with its single bed, was much more to her liking. It was to this room that she took her cases.

For the next hour she was fully occupied with finding linen to make up the single bed, and with emptying her cases of their belongings. This done, the small easy chair in the room beckoned for her to take a few moments' respite. Her hip was beginning to nag—hardly surprising, she thought, since from Wednesday morning onwards she had not had time to take those periods of rest Dr Henekssen had advised she frequently had. And she had done herself no favours by lugging her cases around.

An unexpected sob caught her out, and suddenly she could not bear to be in the alien house any longer. In minutes she had picked up her bag and was slamming the front door behind her.

As if trying to escape the devil, Devon walked quickly the good mile to the outskirts of Marchworth proper. And it was there, in the first café she came to, that she found rest from the toothache in her hip, and a semblance of calm from what she now realised had been panic that had been in her ever since she had waved her father off—time afterwards to think only of herself.

By the time she had disposed of her second cup of tea, she had given herself a stern lecture on outstanding debts to be paid, accounts to be met. And she was then ready to return to The Limes, if not looking forward to living with Grant Harrington, then at least calmer in the knowledge that by her doing so, her father should know a future that was untroubled.

She made it to the bus stop, to find that she had just missed a bus that would have taken her three parts of the way to her destination. But that semblance of calm was still with her, so she was able to reason that since Grant Harrington had given no specific time when he would reach his home, and since it was only a quarter to five—and if he was back early from wherever he had been, he would most likely go to his office—then she couldn't expect his arrival to be before, say, five-thirty.

Buses to that part of town were not plentiful, though expecting another one to come along any minute, but getting tangled up with the rush hour, it was nearer six when Devon turned her feet up the drive of The Limes.

The long sleek car that stood outside the front door had

the calm she had fought so hard for wanting to bolt—and her along with it. She made herself think of her father, of how different he had been since Grant Harrington's visit on Tuesday; and she had climbed the concrete steps.

Wondering if she should ring the bell and wait to be let in, Devon was again beset by nerves. She decided against calling him to answer the front door—she lived here now, didn't she?—temporarily. Very temporarily, if she had her way.

She entered the house having no idea where in its vastness he would be, and crossed the hall thinking, since he could only just have got in himself, he wouldn't be put out that her timing was off.

In that, as she opened the sitting-room door and went in, she was to discover she had never been more wrong.

She had thought she was calmer, but one look at Grant Harrington's dark expression as he watched her walk in was enough to have all calm departing, and her insides quaking. He was absolutely furious, she saw, and he wasn't about to waste any time in letting her know it!

'Where in sweet hell have you been?' he blazed before she could begin to explain she had missed a bus, but had still thought to be there first. 'I told you to be here when I returned!' he thundered.

CHAPTER SIX

'If this is how you keep your promises,' Grant Harrington continued to rage, 'then they're as worthless as you are!'

That stung, and Devon felt anger she was in no position to feel, as she retorted hotly, 'I don't have a crystal ball—you didn't say what time you would be back. I assumed . . .'

Her voice trailed off as his narrow-eyed gaze took in the flashing blue of hers. But with his words separating themselves in her mind to mean that with her not being there as he had commanded, he saw it as her breaking her word—which left him free to break his if he so wished, she was quickly swallowing down her ire.

'I'm sorry,' she apologised, defensive all of a sudden. 'I missed a bus and had to wait . . .'

'Bus!' She hadn't thought his sarcasm would stay hidden for long. 'I would have thought a taxi far more your style.' Oh, how she hated him, hated him that she had to take a defensive position. 'You mean you actually *walked* a quarter of a mile from the bus stop!'

Anger was needling her off her defensive stance. She was quite well aware that he thought her a lazy slob, without his sarcasm. But all at once, like a sudden flash of blinding light, it came to her that the sooner that *major* promise to him had been kept, the sooner that threat hanging over her father would be lifted—only then would she be able to breathe more easily. As suddenly, all her anger drained away. Though before she could so much as get in there and try to placate him, Grant was there first, sarcasm gone, as he rapped shortly:

'Where's your luggage? I told you to come prepared to stay a while.'

Well, at least she'd got something right. 'I was here earlier,' she told him, not too hopeful of a gold star since his grim expression hadn't lightened at all. 'I put my things upstairs.' And tiptoeing, since it looked as though just one wrong word from her would have him cancelling their contract, 'I didn't think you would mind.'

If he suspected sarcasm behind her words, though in truth she was meaning her taking the liberty of wandering over his home, then a master at trying to kill her with a look, he ordered her to, 'Pour me a Scotch—I'm going up to change.'

Unused to pouring a Scotch measure, Devon went to the drinks cabinet when he had gone, and poured the same quantity she thought she had seen him pour before.

Obviously the sour brute had just got in. Otherwise, it was equally obvious, had she not come in close on his heels, he would either have picked up the phone giving instructions to re-call her father, or, alternatively, have driven over to her home to drag her here by the roots of her hair. Nobody, she guessed, ever welshed on him without paying for it.

Grant Harrington was not upstairs many minutes, but when he returned, there was an ominous tight-lipped look to him that had her quailing again. Having no idea what thoughts had gone through his head while he had been changing, Devon, hating it, again found herself having to be placatory.

Handing him the Scotch she had poured on his instruction, she offered a tentative, 'I hope it's all right,' and excused, 'I wasn't sure of the measure—we only ever have sherry at home.'

Wordlessly he took the drink from her, but the way he

tipped half of it into the water jug, before tipping the other half down his throat, spoke volumes. She didn't doubt, as he served her with a dark look, that he thought this was just another instance of her lying just for the sake of it. But as the empty glass was placed carefully down on a tray, and his voice came, frighteningly quiet, she thought, so all other thought froze in her as he said:

'Come with me.'

Her eyes shot to his. There was danger here, she felt it, could almost touch it. 'Where?' she asked, her voice gone husky.

'Upstairs.'

Just that one word, but it was sufficient to have her feet glued to the ground. Why? she wanted to ask. But she rather thought she knew. Oh God, she had thought it would happen tonight—but dear lord, wasn't he going to wait that long!

Knowing she should be dashing up the stairs ahead of him the sooner to have what was at the root of their bargain sealed, thereby securing his word not to prosecute, Devon felt incapable of moving one step. And that didn't suit Grant Harrington.

His hand crushing the bones in her wrist manacled her as he jerked her to go with him. Pain shot through her hip so that she was having to concentrate hard on not only trying to keep the lid on her panic, but also in not favouring that hip. He had no belief in anything she told him. Should he see her limp and ask the reason, then her truthful answer would have him seeing it as another of her lies—hadn't he threatened to ram such lies back down her throat?—that being achieved, she saw, treading the stairs behind him, her wrist still held, by taking her in anger!

Panic that he would roughly use her was sinking her when they reached the top of the stairs and he had hauled her along the landing behind him. Then panic was mixed with confusion that he wasn't taking her to the room where that ginormous bed was, but was pushing open the door to the room she had selected for herself!

'What's the big idea?' he questioned shortly, swinging her into the room in front of him, only then letting go her wrist.

She stumbled, and because of pain, limped a couple of steps away from him. Her halting gait was noted by him, but he did not refer to it; it was all part of her stumble in his eyes, she saw.

'I thought,' she said, going very carefully, beginning to feel better that it looked as though she had won a reprieve and that he had dragged her there purely because he was annoyed that she had chosen this room, 'that I would have this room.' And, trying desperately hard to be tactful, 'That is, if you don't mind?'

That he did mind, he did not leave her in any doubt. Swiftly he brushed past her and opened the wardrobe door, sarcasm back with him.

'I have every confidence that you've investigated each room in the house,' he said. And cuttingly, as he indicated the contents of the wardrobe, 'You can just take this little lot and put them in the wardrobe I've moved into my room.'

Unreasonable pig! she fumed silently, anger being allowed to surface now that it looked as though she had earned a temporary respite from her worst fear. How the dickens was she supposed to have found a room not in use if it wasn't by investigating?

'Do I really have to move my things?' she asked, trying to get through to him and his unreasonable attitude. 'I mean,' she rushed on when all she received in reply was one of his superior looks, 'it's not—that is—well, I thought it would be all right if I had a room to myself.

You've got plenty to spare,' she thought to point out. 'And
. . . and it's not as if—as if you'll want me with you all
night, is it?'

'Who says I won't?' he asked loftily. And Devon forgot
to be placatory.

'I prefer to sleep alone,' she snapped, having known she
wouldn't be able to keep up her passive role for long.

And never had she felt such violent feelings towards
anyone, when, mockery back, he drawled insolently, 'I'll
bet you say that to all the boys.' His voice went tough
then, when tersely he commanded, 'Get your stuff
moved.'

Hanging grimly on to the temper he had awakened
from sleep, Devon saw she wasn't quick enough to obey
him. For the next thing she knew, long arms had snaked
inside the wardrobe and jeans, dresses and skirts were
more or less thrown at her, with the comment that she had
had too much of her own way in the past and that now she
could damn well do as she was told.

Her arms full, angrily Devon spun away from him, her
hip catching her out, and the ensuing limp bringing forth
the comment she could do without:

'See where being smart gets you!'

Determined not to limp again, though very aware it
might have proved less painful, she walked to the room
she knew was his, not liking that he stood by and watched
as she hung her everyday sort of clothes up.

'You appear to have left your haute couture outfits at
home,' he remarked sourly, having watched her for some
minutes without speaking.

She was not unaware that some of her dresses had faded
from too much washing, but she could have done without
his commentary. Or the fact that he seemed determined to
needle her. Though why he should want to do that was
beyond her. Unless he was hating this situation as much

as her—hating himself, but determined to go through with it.

'Why,' he pressed, when she clamped her lips firmly and refused to be drawn, 'bring only this sort of gear—trying to get me to fork out for something I shan't be ashamed to be seen out with you in?'

Mutinously Devon thought again what a lovely mind he'd got, deciding hotly that he wasn't hating anything but her and what he thought she stood for. If he went to buy her so much as a pair of tights, she'd wrap them around his throat and pull—hard!

'It hadn't occurred to me that we would be going out,' she retorted—and was hard put not to thump him when he taunted:

'You *have* had some strange bedfellows!' He ignored the flame in her eyes at his implication that all she did with her other 'bedfellows' was stay in bed, then announced, his eyes flicking over the rest of her, 'You're passable enough for anyone not to be ashamed to seen out with you,' and as her anger peaked, 'Since shame doesn't come easily to me, I'll take you out in what you're wearing.'

Lofty swine! she thought, as he strolled out, obviously bored standing about watching her stow her things away.

Several trips more were needed to the bedroom she would have preferred, but which had been ruled out by His Mightiness. She investigated a chest of drawers and found that two drawers had been emptied for her use.

In no hurry to join him downstairs, thinking that since it looked as though they were dining out, eight o'clock would be soon enough to go down, Devon then checked that the adjacent bathroom had a bolt on it.

She found the bathwater soothing to her hip, its constant nagging having had a flutter of a different sort of panic invadings. But as the ache was eased away, so she was able to think more rationally. But in remembering that her hip was fine now, and that tomorrow, since Grant Harrington would not want her with him during the day as well, and would probably take himself off somewhere, leaving her able to get in some of that much needed rest, so some of her mutiny against him died. Devon gave herself another talking to.

But it was one thing to know that the sooner she gave herself to him the sooner that threat to her father would be lifted. And quite another, she was quickly realising when a heavy fist hammered on the bathroom door, and a sharp voice called:

'I'm hungry. Get a move on!'

It was something, she supposed, *him* being *him*, that he hadn't attempted to try the door and just barge in to issue his orders. But get a move on she did—just in case—blaming the soothing bathwater that she had lain there without thought to time.

Having thought to bring the clothes she would wear into the bathroom with her, hurriedly Devon dried and got into a dress that admittedly was home-made, but since she was quite expert with her needle, she hoped didn't shriek 'I made it myself'.

She listened at the bathroom door, and not hearing a sound, emerged to find she still had the bedroom to herself. There were other bathrooms in the house, so if Grant Harrington had come up for a shower, he must have showered elsewhere, she thought, though she didn't delay very long.

Lipsticked, powdered, and with the quickest of brushes through her hair, she hurriedly left the bedroom, panicking again that if she didn't soon present herself, that 'I'm hungry' that had been rapped would have his appetite going in other directions.

His damp hair, when she joined him in the sitting room, told Devon her surmise that he had showered elsewhere had been accurate. He was wearing a faintly checked lounge suit, and would, she couldn't help thinking, be the sort of escort, large and distinguished-looking, that many girls might have been thrilled to be seen out with—though not her.

His eyes went over her blue dress, the colour bringing out the brilliance of her eyes. 'Do you always take this long to get ready?' he asked belligerently, for all there was an admiration showing in his glance she found unnerving.

'Doesn't every girl?' she asked huskily—and was grateful that he didn't deign to answer as he moved to the door and she followed him out to his car.

Like every girl she wanted to be pretty, beautiful even, as Grant had remarked she was. But as effortlessly he swung the car out of the drive, without having the least idea what it was about her that clearly drew him to desire her, as her feet got colder and colder, so Devon was wishing that it was something she had been born without.

Feeling a mass of contradictions, for how could she think that way when because of either that certain something—or maybe because Grant Harrington was hellbent on making her pay for once in her life—she should be glad she was to be used to keep her father safe from prison. But as thoughts that she would have to lie with this bear of a man at her side throughout the night started to make her jittery, as he pulled the car up outside a smart and lively-looking club, so Devon, not used to contact with strangers anyway, shrank within herself.

She was aware of eyes turning in their direction as the head waiter guided them to their table, but she had eyes for nowhere but in front of her.

Without taking any of it in, she read the menu. And she did not miss the glint in Grant's eyes that said he thought she was just being difficult when she couldn't make up her mind what she wanted to eat.

'Anything will do,' she said, thinking anything would just about choke her.

'Are you dieting?' he asked shortly, when she had only picked at her starter, and wasn't making very much of a job of the chicken in wine sauce in front of her.

'I never diet,' she replied stiffly, nerves jumping again as that brought his eyes to give a cursory but well documented glance to what he could see of her figure.

'Then eat,' he rapped sharply, flushing out a nervous anger as she snapped back:

'I'm not hungry.'

Taking her at her word that she never had cause to diet, she heard him order a chocolate nut meringue for her final course—which, when delivered to the table, looked absolutely delicious, but which, after the first spoonful, had her knowing, as her stomach consumed by nerves revolted, that she would be in trouble if she ate any more.

Without fuss, she laid down her spoon, and because she had to look somewhere, she directed her eyes on to the dance area below them. Perhaps, she thought, trying to latch on to something pleasant, when all this was over, she might get invited out by some more agreeable man. It would be lovely to dance like those people down there. She twisted in her seat to get a better look at the steps they were doing, and was reminded that she wasn't yet up to such energetic gyrations when she felt a twinge in her hip.

She would definitely try and rest tomorrow, she was just thinking, when her thoughts were abruptly cut into by Grant, who must have observed her preoccupation with those on the dance floor.

'We'll dance,' he said—no 'would you care to' about it!

'I don't . . .' she said, her head turning to see he was already on his feet. She had been in his arms twice before, but her nerves jangled; all too soon she would be in them again. 'I don't dance,' she told him chokily.

That he sat down and wasn't pressing when she could see from his glinting eyes that her confession had been received as a blatant lie, and she knew she would soon be on the receiving end of a few pertinent comments; they were not very long in coming.

'I've just about had it with you, Devon Johnston,' he said, his anger barely leashed. 'You might hate my guts that for the first time in your life you're not getting something for free. But just remember this,' he went on, the leash on his temper straining as he leaned forward and snarled in a low tone, '*I* didn't ask your father to steal from me. By your own admission he did it for *you*. So you just damn well enter into the right spirit—or,' he threatened, which had fear for her father mixing in with the rest of her nerves, 'you'll find it won't take me above two minutes to telegraph Scotland!'

Her voice stuck somewhere deep in her throat, Devon wanted to tell him she had every intention of entering into the right spirit. But he wouldn't believe her anyway if she did tell him that truly she didn't dance, she saw. Though before she could get vocal release to try and tell him anyhow, the most stunning of sophisticated redheads appeared as if from nowhere at their table.

'Grant—darling!' she exclaimed, causing Devon to be grateful to her, for her exclamation had his aggressive look going from her, and changing as he rose to his feet while the redhead carried on, 'I tried to get you at your office, but they said you were in France.'

'For a few days only,' he replied, a glimmer of a smile on his face, but anger about him still; that smile did not reach his eyes, Devon noted.

'I rang wanting to ask you to join Noel's birthday celebrations tonight,' the redhead went on, flicking a bright glance in Devon's direction. 'Won't you—and your friend, of course—join our party?'

Not sure whether she wanted him to say yes or no, suddenly aware that her dress must shriek 'home-made' after all beside the elegance of the redhead's slinky outfit, Devon thought it might delay for a few hours what was before her.

'My salutations to Noel,' she heard Grant courteously declining, 'but you'll forgive me, Vivien,' he said urbanely, 'Miss Johnston informs me she wants an early night.'

He's furious, Devon thought, as, not introducing her to his redheaded friend, though with a charm she had never suspected him of having, he insisted quite firmly that he was taking Miss Johnston home.

He had not one word to say to her as the car sped in the direction of The Limes. Nor did he have a word to say to her, as together they went up the steps to the house and he inserted his key in the door.

And Devon knew then, afraid to say a word to placate him in case it had the opposite effect and angered him further, that when it would have been perhaps easier for her if he had claimed his retribution with thought for her, she didn't have a hope that that was the way it would be. It was at that point that her brain seized up.

The hall lights had been switched on, illuminating the staircase. But, fearful that at any moment Grant Harrington was going to make a grab for her—the knowledge deep-rooted by now that she dared not make any protest if she didn't want that cable on its way to Scotland—Devon stood petrified, not knowing which way to go, or if she should move at all.

But even so, she was in no mind to thank him, when Grant, not making the grab for her she had been expecting, looked her cynically over from top to toe, then gave her direction.

'You know where my bedroom is,' he grunted tersely, and left her standing as he strode to the sitting room,

effectively barring her way by closing the door behind
him. But still she hesitated as she looked from that door to
the staircase, that to her suddenly weakened limbs looked
to be a mile high.

Her father—she had to think of her father, she thought,
when in turning, her eyes caught sight of the front door and
escape. She moved to the foot of the stairs clutching at the
banister, needing a moment to find strength not to do
what all her instincts were urging. Grant Harrington
would most likely hear her if she exited from that front
door—but he would make no move to come after her and
haul her back—he had no need to, all the high cards were
his. Slowly Devon began to ascend the stairs.

It was impossible, she found, to keep her mind the
blank she wanted it. But with the picture in front of her of
her father before and after Grant Harrington's visit to him
on Tuesday, she found it a help in pushing that word
escape to the back of her mind as she washed, and
changed into her short cotton nightdress.

The bed, when she made herself climb into it, seemed
enormous. But even so, as another flutter of panic came to
swamp her, she didn't doubt that Grant Harrington
would find her.

She had felt exhausted earlier, was tired still, she
admitted. But, when sleep would have been a welcome
relief from her tortured thoughts, as she turned out the
bedside lamp and the room went dark, her alarm was too
great for sleep to be anywhere near.

Her nerves jumpy in the darkness for any sound, having
already had several false alarms, Devon had her work cut
out to stay exactly where she was when this time the
muffled sounds she heard, were followed by a firm tread
outside the door. Then the door of the room she was in
opened!

Oh God, she prayed as she heard Grant quietly close

the door after him, please don't let me back away. He did
not put on the light, but she sensed from his quiet
deliberate movements that he was still furious with her—
no need for her to see his face to know that.

Praying as hard as she could that instinct would not
make her fight him when he came near, knowing he would
see that as him being cheated a second time, when he
would either rape her, or leave her to order her father's
recall, when as morning came he would start legal pro-
ceeding, Devon began to wilt under the weight of her
thoughts.

Then she was having to fight with all she had against
the instinct that would have her shooting out of bed, for a
movement on the covers at the other side told her that she
was about to have company.

She had already started to tremble, and he had not
touched her yet. But by the time she felt him with her
beneath those covers, she was shaking so badly, he just
had to feel it.

He knew she was awake, could not help knowing, she
thought, wishing she could still the dreadful shaking that
had taken her. But he was wasting no time, when wordlessly he did nothing to help by stretching out one long,
muscled, naked arm and drawing her to him.

'Adding actress to your other attributes, Devon?' he
asked as he pulled her trembling form yet closer. And
when she couldn't answer him, curtly he told her, 'Stow
it—you're going to be mine, with, or without the melo-
drama!'

And as a follow-up to that, he raised himself till his
naked chest was over hers. And while she was panicking—
Oh, dear God, she had never seen a man naked in her
life—she was now in bed with a man who, by the feel of his
bare legs touching hers, had not a stitch on, he was
brutally assaulting her lips with his.

'Don't!' she objected, twisting her face from his. And she felt him tense, as he gritted in sudden fury:

'Don't?'

Devon knew then that this was her last chance. One wrong word or movement from her and whichever was the greater of the two evils, and she owned she wasn't thinking very coherently just then, would befall either her or her father.

Thoughts of her father had her quickly, if stammeringly, telling him, 'I m-meant—don't—be—rough with me.'

His harsh laugh told her he considered she was still play-acting. 'That'll be up to you,' he grunted. Then his lips were again over hers.

Unresponsive, willing herself not to pull away, Devon lay still while he kissed her again, his mouth trailing to her throat. She tensed when she felt his hands come to caress her shoulders. And she was swallowing great gulps of air when just before his mouth returned to hers, she felt his hands, warm on her waist, begin a caressing movement upwards.

So far her hands had not touched him, but when she felt them at her breasts, so the need swamped her to hang on to something. And she was panicking as never before when his hands caressed and seemed to be quite happy to linger over the peaks that ended her swollen roundness.

For a moment as again he claimed her mouth her hands shot up to clutch at him. But when an awareness came that she was touching the naked skin of his back, so her hands fell away.

A fresh shaking possessed her when as his lips did a sortie to her chest, he must have felt frustration that the neck of her nightdress prevented him from more intimate access to her bosom. For before she could know what he was about, he had found the hem of her nightdress, and with experienced movements, he had pulled it over her head with the dry comment of, 'You won't be needing this,' and she discovered that she was naked.

It was instinct alone that was her mentor then, as without being aware that she had moved, she had edged away from him as if trying to escape. But Grant had quickly hauled her back, the time gone when he had left the choice to go or to stay with her.

She felt his hair-roughened chest over her, and quite simply, she froze. Something inside her was trying to get through to tell her that it would be far better for her if she could reciprocate. But she was too numbed for any such intelligence to get through.

Grant's kisses were becoming of a more passionate nature, his hands on her frightening her to death as they touched her flat belly before going to her waist. And then both his hands and his lips were caressing her naked breasts, fiercely, as though he was being goaded by her lack of response.

Then suddenly he was pulling away, his voice angry as he growled, 'Respond, damn you! I want to make love to a woman, not a piece of wood!'

'I'm—sorry,' she said chokily, tears near to the surface. And fear was there still, as she told him, 'I am—trying.'

Whether he thought she was still acting, she had no way of knowing. But suddenly, the next time he kissed her, his kiss was different. There was none of the experience he had in that gentle kiss as, his hands nowhere near her now, he tenderly pressed on her mouth a giving kiss that sought nothing. And, as gently his mouth lay over hers, all at once Devon knew confusion.

When he kissed her again in much the same way, though his kiss was longer this time, there seemed something in it that magically had her trembling vanishing. And when, for a third time, gently he kissed her, so she discovered that one of her hands had strayed up to the side of his face in a kind of supplication.

His mouth was still over hers when with unhurried movements, very tenderly his hands moved to caress her midriff.

'Your skin is like satin,' he murmured softly, the aggression she had feared far from him now.

And strangely, she found herself glad that he thought her skin like satin, as his whispered caresses became more intimate and her breasts were gently moulded until the tips turned hard in his hands.

Again his hands caressed over her, as again his lips met hers. And when a different sort of trembling began to make itself felt in her, Devon was in a quagmire of confusion—for that trembling had not come from fear.

Though she was to know fear again, when with another softly breathed comment about the satinness of her skin, Grant turned her until she was on her side. And she was once more beset by nerves to feel her body moved as he pulled her closer, so that for the first time in her life she was lying skin to naked skin against a warm, vibrant male.

Her reaction was swift, scared, and immediate. 'Oh!' she cried, as rapidly she backed from him.

She heard his raw breath, and as hard hands gripped at her, she knew she had messed it up. Had she continued to respond in the way she had been, she suddenly realised that if that was what she wanted, then Grant would have taken her gently.

But his male aggression was soaring, because it looked as though she had responded so far but only to lead him on, and that she was playing some teasing game—and it was then his patience disappeared.

Aggression riding him, he was no longer paying heed to gentleness, tenderness, or any other consideration he had

shown her. And it was with a rough movement that he
yanked her back against him.

Her hip was not up to being jerked so suddenly, and a
small cry of pain left her as it let her know about it. And it
was a moan of pain Grant heard, as with his hand still on
her hip, and sounding as though he wasn't going to believe
her if this was some ruse, he asked in the darkness:

'What was that about?'

'I—did—did ask you—not to be rough with me,' she
choked, as his hand began a not so absent backward and
forward movement over her hip where, had he not been so
incensed, he would have felt that the skin was far from
satiny.

Devon felt his face close to hers once more. And she
knew she would soon be on the receiving end of one of his
earlier, experienced kisses.

But then, all at once, his head was pulling back. And it
was just as if the word she had used, that word 'rough' had
just got through to him. For suddenly he had stilled, his
only movement the fingers of his left hand as they found
the line of her recent scar. Devon felt him tense, and then
with agonising slowness, as if he couldn't believe what he
was feeling, deliberately, he traced from top to bottom the
long, long outline of her scar.

He stilled again when he had finished, then, 'What in
hell . . .' she heard him mutter.

Then in the next second he had jerked to suddenly sit
upright, and light was flooding the bed area as he flicked
on the bedside lamp. And regardless, as he threw the
covers from her naked form, that she was going all shades
of pink, ending with a livid scarlet, Grant stared hard and
long at the three scars that came over her right hip and
ended some way down her thigh.

'Good God almighty!' she heard him breathe, as still he
stared as though not believing his eyes.

But it was not many seconds before he was getting to grips with his shock. And his voice had gone hard, his jaw jutting grimly, as tersely he instructed:

'Sit up—and start talking!'

CHAPTER SEVEN

SENSING that the shock he had received had banished his desire for the moment, Devon struggled to sit up as Grant had ordered.

She saw his steady look go from her scars and over skin which was more satiny. But she was relieved that he had no objection to make when she took hold of the bedclothes and covered part of him and the front of her. That he was unashamed of his nudity helped her to come to terms with seeing his broad uncovered chest not a yard away.

'One of those scars is recent,' he said sharply, when she took too long to start talking.

'I—told you all about it,' she reminded him.

'How recent?' he persisted. And she saw, while there was nothing the matter with his memory, she was convinced of that, that he wanted it all, chapter and verse again.

'I had a—tricky hip,' she said flatly. 'I was operated on in Sweden two months ago.'

She dared a look at him and was pierced, hypnotised by dark frowning eyes. That stunned look had left him, she saw, and she just knew, when he continued to frown as he kept his eyes on her, that he was backtracking over everything she had ever told him.

'I was telling you the truth,' she said in a sudden rush, feeling hot when his eyes went from her face to her shoulder that peeped out from the covers.

She thought she read desire spurting to his eyes. And she had the knowledge then that he still wanted her, the knowledge that, for whatever reason her father had taken that money, Grant Harrington still wanted his retribution.

Her throat went dry and she looked away from him as his hand came out, instinct making her grab at the sheet when it fell away. She recaptured the sheet, but his hand came over hers and stayed her movement, his hand still over hers as it rested on her breast.

Feeling shaky, her heart going like a trip hammer, Devon reached the end of her tether at last. Her father was in danger still, she wanted it all over and done with.

'I'm willing to—co-operate,' she said huskily, bravely raising her eyes to his. Her colour was warm as his hand burned over hers, the flame in his eyes scorching her as she rushed on in nervous speech. 'I'm sorry about—about just now. I—I didn't meant to back away—only—only—well . . . And I wouldn't have cried out, only . . .'

She took a deep breath, trying for control, knowing she was gabbling on and that it wasn't words he wanted from her, but action.

'K-kiss me, Grant,' she said—and nearly died with embarrassment at the brazenness of her request, when for a moment it looked, as his head came nearer, as though he would do exactly that. But he did not kiss her, choosing instead to pull abruptly back, his eyes still showing the heat of his desire for her, as his other hand came up to crush her shoulder as he growled:

'Why *did* you cry out?'

She saw no point in prevarication—they had come too far for that. 'I felt a bit of a niggle in my hip when you . . .'

'When I got tough and didn't care much for you backing off?' he questioned, his eyes narrowing.

'It was only a niggle,' she repeated, and, nervous still, 'I—haven't rested much t-today.'

Sharply he looked at her, his jaw jutting as he remembered, and sounding accusing, he said, 'You were limping earlier. Were you in pain then?'

'It was only from sudden movement,' she replied. 'I'm . . .'

'You once told me your doctor had told you not to overstrain—what? Your hip?'

Having gone through numerous emotions that night, Devon was suddenly starting to grow fed up that, now she had conditioned herself to accept what she could not escape, Grant Harrington was going to dissect every word she had ever said to him.

'What does it matter?' she asked.

And she knew then, as he looked at her as though he did not care for her tone, that he thought she was right, that they were wasting time, and that nothing mattered but that his desire for her body should be eased.

'So—co-operate,' he said harshly. Then he hauled her up against him, moving her before she was ready. Devon did not cry out this time when her hip protested, but the way she suddenly clutched on to him said it all.

Grant Harrington looked as fed up as she had previously felt, when with a frustrated grunt he threw her away from him, and with a muttered but clear pronouncement of, 'This is bloody ridiculous!' that revealed all his frustration, careless that she had full view of his long lean-limbed nakedness as he turned his back on her, he got up from the bed.

She looked away, but saw when he strode angrily to the door that he had shrugged into a robe. Though she had to know, if the way the door slammed after him was anything to go by, that either he was violently angry with himself for having deprived himself when she had offered herself to him on a plate, or he was furious with her that by revealing her pain, she had stirred a sensitivity in him he did not want to feel.

For an age after he had gone, Devon lay there wondering if he would have second thoughts and come back. She wasn't at all sure how she felt about that. For having got round to thinking about how she had felt inside when he had gently begun to make love to her, she wasn't sure she was not just a little disgusted with herself. For how could it be that a man she had such loathing for should be capable of making her feel sensuous pleasure?

As more minutes ticked by and she was uninterrupted in the big bed, so she began to relax. Exhaustion crept in, weariness taking over. She was on the point of discounting that Grant Harrington had any sensitivity at all, when she fell asleep.

It was broad daylight when she awakened, and for a moment she did not know where she was. Then as she sat up and looked around and saw that she still had the big bed all to herself, so everything that had taken place rushed in.

My God! she thought, uppermost in her mind the memory that she had actually felt the first stirrings of desire in her, when that hateful man had put himself out to gently woo her.

Hastily she got out of bed, and was in the bathroom before it occurred to her that she did not have one single solitary niggle in her hip this morning.

By the time she was showered and was dressed in a light summer frock, Devon had relived every part of the previous evening. But by then it was not the memory of the feeling Grant Harrington's expertise had aroused in her when he had begun gently kissing her that was large in her mind; but thoughts that now she had told him that *she* wanted to co-operate—her father was still not out of the wood until Grant Harrington *too* had co-operated!

She found him in the kitchen frying bacon and eggs when she went downstairs. But the flick of a glance she received in greeting was sufficient to tell her that although it was a beautiful day outside, the sun had not risen with his world this morning.

'Er—good morning,' she said, pink in her cheeks that he was too busy with the frying pan to notice.

Her blush deepened that she was ignored. With a feeling of not staying where she wasn't wanted, Devon turned about and would have gone swiftly to another room.

'Breakfast will be ready in a minute,' Grant grunted as she reached the doorway.

She turned, observing he had flicked another sour glance at her, noting what she had been about, and still ready with his orders—albeit that his order had been veiled, an order that she should not leave the kitchen.

'Can I do anything to help?' she asked, resigned again as she left the doorway and went back into the streamlined, last-word-in-modern-equipment kitchen.

His sarcasm she should have expected, she realised. But she was annoyed nevertheless, when, either thinking she was some ninety-year-old granny, or having come round to being sceptical about her performance last night, he threw over his shoulder not the answer she was expecting, but:

'How are your aches and pains this morning?'

'I wasn't lying to you last night to get out of . . .' she started to flare—but was made to go on as he turned, one eyebrow going insolently aloft as though to say, tell me more. 'I—want to—as much as you . . .' again she faltered. 'Where do you keep your cutlery?' she snapped, going red. 'This table wants laying.'

He smirked, she was sure he did. Even if there wasn't a

smirk about him as he pointed to the cutlery drawer and said, 'Want to play housewife?'

'I kept house for my father,' she told him sharply. And just in case he was going to belittle that, 'And very efficiently too,' she tacked on. And she slammed knives and forks down, one knife bouncing to the floor to prove her inefficient.

'Visitors,' he said, and suddenly her ill humour had gone, and her lips were twitching that he knew the old saying that a dropped knife meant visitors.

Of course, her face instantly went into straight lines when she caught him looking at the curve to her mouth. She didn't want to be amused by any unexpected thing he said. Solemn-faced, she checked that the table had every-thing they would need. And then as Grant placed two plates of bacon and egg down on the table, she realised she was starving, and did not need a second invitation to:

'Sit down and tuck in.'

He was quite good with a frying pan, she thought, not being small-minded, deciding to give him credit for some-thing. She stood up when her bacon and eggs had been demolished, and held her hand out for his cleared plate. A piece of toast and a dab of marmalade would finish the meal off nicely, she thought, resuming her seat after depositing their used plates on the draining board. But then she heard, having thought he didn't like conversa-tion with his first meal of the day, that Grant Harrington had more than one or two questions he wanted to put to her.

'Why,' he asked for starters, as she selected a piece of toast from the toast rack, 'do you "want to" as much as I?'

Blankly she looked at him, then she went off all idea of wanting a piece of toast. She would have preferred that he had chosen any other subject for a breakfast time discussion than that one.

Feeling pink about the ears that he must have felt her response to him last night—however small—and might somehow have got the impression she was hot for him, she was quick to knock that idea straight out of his head.

'Why, because of my father, of course,' she replied.

And looking at him and seeing that he didn't look brokenhearted, not that that would have worried her, she told him more than she had to, in the faint hope that when he knew, he might yet say that in the circumstances he couldn't possibly prosecute, that her father was free, and so was she.

'While I'm still a . . .' the word stuck, '. . . a virgin, you have a hold on my father,' she explained, an unconscious note of appeal in her voice.

'You're a *virgin*!' His exclamation had her eyes shooting to him, wonder in her, as she saw his stunned look, that she hadn't thought to tell him that before—though he wouldn't have believed her then, would he? 'Ye gods,' he said, and she could see he was getting over his surprise, and wasn't ready to believe her even now, as he added shortly, 'With your looks—that's rich!'

Swine, she thought, not for the first time, and vowed then that he'd have to put her on the rack before she would tell him anything else.

'It is, isn't it,' she said coldly, and set about spreading butter on a piece of toast she didn't want.

She had the toast halfway to her mouth, when the lengthy silence coming from the other end of the table made her look at him. And it seemed to her then that he was going over her every action with him in that big bed last night. For his eyes were going from her eyes to her mouth, and as her hand started to shake so that she returned the toast to her plate and put her hands in her lap out of sight, she just knew that he was remembering her trembling, and was now accepting, when adding the way she had been to what she had just told him, that her trembling was not an act, but that she had been scared stiff.

For all of two seconds she forgot to hate him. She very nearly smiled, when for all of two seconds he proved that he was after all a gentleman, and a man who would not rob an innocent girl of her virginity.

'You can forget all your fears for your father, Devon,' he said, and there was a great deal of the charm she had seen him use on the stunning Vivien last night, as, his look wry, he smiled.

Her mouth wanted to pick up at the corners that clearly he was telling her that her father was saved without the diabolical need for her again to sleep in that over-large bed.

But—there was something about the look in his eyes that, while joy leapt in her heart, some cautionary instinct was there to remind her that once before she had been ready to kiss him enthusiastically for his goodness—only to discover very shortly afterwards that he was more devil than saint.

'You mean . . . ?' she questioned, that hope buoyantly alive, hope still on top.

'I mean, my dear Devon,' he smiled, 'that since you've confessed yourself so willing to—co-operate—why then should you worry about your father's fate?' And while her hope started to die, Grant Harrington made it abundantly plain what he meant, as with not a smile about him, he said, 'To put it more bluntly, Miss Johnston, virgin you may be now—but not for very much longer.'

Warm colour flared to her face. She felt let down, though she was not sure why she should feel so. She had known the score from the start and if given the same choice, she would still have taken the same course. Grant Harrington might have left her alone last night because of her nagging hip, but that did not mean the contract was made null and void. And whether she was a virgin or not, it was all the same to him—nothing was altered by that fact.

'That—er . . .' She coughed to clear her throat, hating that he was witnessing her nervousness. 'That,' she said more firmly, 'goes without saying.'

In moody silence they shared the chore of the washing up. Then when, to her relief, he seemed to have a need to work off some of his excess energy and went outside to mow the lawns, Devon took herself off upstairs.

She had taken her time in generally tidying the bed-room and the bathroom, when she suddenly became aware that the mower had stopped. She wasted no time in leaving the bedroom, though she was to meet Grant halfway on the staircase.

Not missing his sardonic look, she would have passed him without a word. But he murmured softly, 'You *have* been mixing with the wrong company!' just as if to say that he knew why she had bolted from the bedroom, but that he was not the type to grab whenever an opportunity presented itself. It had her replying acidly as he went up one stair and she went down one:

'Only recently.'

And, when the exchange had not been funny, she couldn't help, as she continued down where he could not see her face, that her lips should twitch to hear him smother what surely had been a laugh at her matching sarcasm, as he tossed after her:

'I'll take mine black—without sugar!'

He had joined her in the kitchen by the time she had the coffee made. And it was he who found a tray and loaded it, and said, 'We'll have this in the sitting room.' And it was Grant who carried the tray through, making her feel redundant as she wondered, since they didn't have a lot in common, what on earth they would talk about.

She spotted a newspaper on the arm of a chair as he placed the tray down; and was hopeful, as she daintily poured out two cups and handed one to him, that perhaps he would bury himself in newsprint.

'The paper's come,' she said in a broad hint, as she sat in one easy chair and he settled himself back in another.

'So tell me more.'

'More?' she enquired, having not an idea what he was meaning. 'More—of what?'

'Of how you, Devon Johnston, possessor of more than your fair share of . . .' his eyes skimmed over her, 'everything,' he drawled, 'come to be the ripe old age of nearly twenty-two, if your father's personnel record is right,' so he had done some checking up? 'and yet have still managed to steer clear of half the panting males in March-worth.'

He could only be referring to the fact that she had told him she was a virgin, she thought, not wanting this conversation, thinking that if she didn't answer, he might tire of it. But that was before he went on to be more personal, adding when he could see from the hostile look she threw him that it was to be a one-sided conversation:

'Scared you might be, but you're certainly not frigid!'

That he had picked that much up from the way his gentleness had stirred her made Devon want to refute it hotly. But that would be one time when he would know for sure that she was lying.

'I didn't—go in for—boy-friends,' she was forced to confess. And she started to hate him again, not sure when she had ever stopped, as she saw from his doubting expression that he did not believe she had never had a boy-friend, and that he thought she and the truth were enemies still. Tartly, she told him, 'If you must know, I had an—an unsightly limp—before my last operation. I preferred to stay at home.'

She flicked him a look of dislike that he had got that out of her. But she saw in that flick of a glance that though he was sitting with one leg crossed over the other, and looking the epitome of a man relaxed in easy conversation, there was an alert look to his eyes. Though she was glad to note that he had left the subject that would have had her blushing at any minute had he continued, even if she didn't care that he now seemed set to find out more about her old injury.

'Your hip cause you pain?' he enquired, his voice quiet, casual.

'Occasionally,' she muttered in understatement.

'You were in pain the first night I called at your home? That was the reason you appeared to be lolling about on the settee?'

'I . . .' She tried to think back. Had she been in pain? She often had been, so most likely she had been then. 'Probably,' she said—and recalling how impolite she must have seemed, not wanting sympathy for her pain if Grant was thinking of extending it, though that was doubtful, 'I didn't mean to be rude that night, only,' by the very fact he was saying nothing, but was waiting, patiently by his look, for her to continue, had the words forcing themselves out, 'only I wasn't—walking too well, and . . . and whenever I went to stand, it always took me a couple of seconds to get my balance.'

She wouldn't look at him as the silence stretched. She wondered if she had said too much. He couldn't possibly be interested in what she had been like those few months ago. But in that, she found herself mistaken.

'You didn't want some unknown man to see you the way you were?'

'I hated anyone to see me the way I was,' she agreed. 'I hated meeting strangers. M-my father understood about it. And, ordinarily, he would never have brought you into the room where I was, but—but he was so shaken to see you at the front door that for once in all his caring for me, he forgot about me and my—hang-up.'

Silence again, and she still wouldn't look at him. That was until, for the very first time she felt some sort of understanding in him when his voice came, quietly, and he said:

'It was a very real hang-up, wasn't it, Devon?'

She flicked another glance at him, and saw that he was still relaxed, but that there was no hardness in his face. And though she did not want to talk about it, she found herself thinking, as she looked away, that maybe if she told him a little more that he would understand a little too why her father had felt compelled to do what he had.

'The doctor said it had something to do with the fact that my mother was killed in the car accident that left me injured,' she told him, and confessed, 'Though he was of the opinion that I would have overcome what had happened by the time I was eighteen.'

'But you didn't,' he slipped in. But he did not wait for her answer as he went on to ask, 'How old were you when this accident occurred?'

'Fifteen and a half.'

'Your mother was driving the car?'

Devon shook her head. 'My father was,' she said, and quickly, 'But it wasn't his fault.' Then, going on more slowly, 'Although he has suffered agonies from it.'

'Your father was injured too?'

She heard surprise there that he should not be aware of any such injury, and again she shook her head. 'Not physically,' she said. 'But he lost my mother, and he loved her very much.' And all of a sudden it was important in her view that Grant should see that her father had suffered enough pain, and she told him, 'Apart from losing my mother, every day he had the reminder of the accident in me, in the way I walked, in the way I could never get out of a chair and get going until my hip let me know it was all right to move.'

She looked at him as she came to an end. She had been truthful and honest—and hopeful. But when she saw his face, his expression serious, casual no longer, so her spirits dipped. He was looking harsh again, she saw, and knew she could have saved her breath in trying to get him to understand how her father had done what he had.

'My father only took the money because . . .' she went to try again—only to be sharply interrupted by a question that called her honesty into doubt as well as her father's.

'Did you never wonder from where he found that amount of money—or did you know?'

'Of course I didn't know,' she replied, annoyed as much by his sharp tone as by his question. 'He told me . . .' She didn't want to go on, but again, by the silence coming from the other chair, she had to. 'He told me that an— endowment in my name had matured on my twenty-first birthday.' And hating to add liar to her father's short list of crimes, she said quickly, 'But he only did it for me. I've kept him poor paying out all he had for treatments, but he knew what this operation could do for me—if it proved successful. He would never . . .'

'*If* it proved successful.' Sharply she was cut off. 'Is there some doubt?' he rapped.

'No,' she was quick to deny. 'That's to say, I've had a few panicky moments about it,' and more than enough panicky moments where you're concerned, she thought, and had the chance then to explain, 'That first night I came home, I was expecting to find my father in the sitting room. When I clutched on to you, it was because I was showing off the new me to him in my first pair of high heels—only I forgot, I hadn't been practising twists and turns in hospital—it hurt, and I lost my balance,' she said with rueful remembrance. 'And I thought for a panicky moment that the operation was a failure. But,' she went on, that happily out of the way, 'after years of trekking to consulting rooms, I have just one last appointment four weeks on Monday, and then,' she said, unable to stop her eyes from shining, 'I've been assured that I'll be able to do absolutely everything I've ever wanted to do!'

That alert look was still with him when, her eyes shining still, she looked across and saw that his eyes were steady on her. But the shine left her eyes when he suggested coolly, sarcasm, disbelief only in him, she thought:

'Meantime—you've been advised not to overstrain that hip?'

'As a matter of fact,' said Devon, her chin tilting, her voice cold, 'yes.'

She saw his eyes narrow at her cold tone, and was not altogether surprised to hear him jibe:

'Now isn't that just too bad!'

And she had been afraid of his sympathy! She should get to be so lucky. 'Not really,' she said, following his train of thought, pride about all she had. 'As well as telling me to rest frequently, Dr Henekssen told me that exercise is good for me.'

She was back to wanting to thump him when he stood up and, looking ready to return to his labours in the garden, loftily reminded her:

'But you exercised too much yesterday. And in consequence we *both* suffered for it.'

By the time darkness fell that night, Devon was beginning to think that thumping did not begin to nearly cover what she would like to do to Grant Harrington!

It had been he who had cooked their lunch. He who had cooked the dinner they had just consumed. And she was just about sick and tired of having him bossing her about.

Nerves, she knew, had a lot to do with the way she was feeling. For just as he had refused to allow her to do anything that day, telling her mockingly that he didn't want her wearing herself out with the wrong sort of activity, he had just refused to allow her to do the washing up, telling her it wouldn't run away if it was left until the morning.

Ushered into the sitting room, she felt mutinous when Grant told her to go and sit down, while he went to the tape deck and busied himself with sorting out the tape he wanted.

Mutiny started to die when the soft strains of some light air wafted around the room. She had heard of soft lights and sweet music, and as what she saw as a seduction scene was coming up, she needed to change into another gear to be ready to meet it.

'Dance?'

She looked up. Grant was standing over her. Here we go, she thought, trying not to gulp. But she couldn't move.

'I don't dance,' she said huskily.

'I know,' he said, believing her tonight, when last night he had thought her to be lying. And he actually smiled. 'But I promise I won't spring any sudden twists or turns.'

It wasn't the unexpected charm of him that made her get to her feet, she knew that it wasn't. She was sure it was the music getting to her, that and an all-consuming desire to know what it was like to dance, that had her leaving her chair and standing awkwardly in front of him.

'It's easy,' he said softly, his arms coming out for her, 'just follow me.'

And it was easy. And for a few short minutes, or that was how long it seemed, she was in heaven as Grant guided her around the room in her first dance. That he held her firmly, but not tightly, made her forget the fears she had had last night when he had asked her to dance.

'That was—I enjoyed it,' she said, trying to sober down, when all too soon the music ended.

'Want to try another?' he asked, indulgently she thought, when guessing her eyes had told him she had thought her first dance the 'heavenly' she had refrained from saying.

'Please,' she said simply. And soon she was in his arms again, feeling the same wonderful sensation. She was actually dancing. Dancing, *her* with that once tricky hip!

The look on her face when the second tape ended told him she wouldn't object if he went to put on a third. But when, with his arms still around her, he did not ask this time if she wanted to try another, but looked down into her eager face, that feeling of being strangely happy left her. And her heart was bumping madly, when keeping one arm around her, he turned her in the direction of the door and said:

'I think it's time you were in bed.'

Quickly she looked away so he should not read the fear in her eyes and be angered by it. She did not want him angry with her. She wanted him to stay gentle. That way she could . . .

'Yes, of course,' she said.

She was not surprised when he went with her from the sitting room, putting lights out as they went, apparently in no more of a rush to reach the top of the stairs than she was, as with his arm still about her slowly they climbed upwards.

But what did surprise her, indeed had her looking at him with wide eyes when at the door of his room she halted, expecting him to open it for them to go through, was that he should halt too, but make no move to open the door. Suddenly he said instead, that usual note of mockery in his voice:

'Are you sure this doctor chap hasn't already given you the okay to do anything you care to?'

'I'm—p-positive,' she stammered, nowhere near certain of what was going on now, not at all sure of what he was saying until, his look all at once rueful, he said:

'Hell!' And as her face went pink, for that 'Hell!' had to mean he was deciding something connected with making love to her, he was observing her heightened colour, and telling her, 'I swear you must be the first female I've ever caused to blush!'

Gently then he took her in his arms. And it was gently that he kissed her. And because this was the way it had to be, notwithstanding that somehow Grant Harrington was setting off the strangest feelings of her not objecting at all to being kissed by him, when his kiss broke, Devon found her voice, choky though it was, to tell him:

'Th-there's a first time for—everything, Grant.'

She saw a flame light his eyes at her tone, at what she said, at the husky way she had used his first name. But still he made no move to open that door. Then he was taking a pace back from her.

'Not for you there isn't,' he said. 'Not tonight.'

Astonished, for surely all the resting that had been forced on her that day had been with a view to her being on top form at this moment, she stared wide-eyed at him.

Then he was turning her to face the room she had

yesterday selected for herself, his voice gritty, mockery no longer there, as he told her to:

'Take yourself and those baby blue eyes to another room, Devon. I want a bed that fits me tonight.'

CHAPTER EIGHT

'HERE'S a nice cup of coffee for you, Miss Johnston.'

Devon came away from the glumness of her thoughts to see that Mrs Podmore, Grant's Monday to Friday, nine till noon daily, was still cosseting her by bringing out her elevenses to the sun lounger where she lay.

Knowing it was less than useless to protest that she was quite able to get her own coffee, and make Mrs Podmore a cup too if she fancied one, Devon said a polite, 'Thank you, Mrs Podmore,' and that good lady, seeing that the convalescent seemed disposed not to want to talk, went back indoors. With no mind to the coffee placed on the table beside her, Devon went back to her not so happy thoughts.

She had been at The Limes for over a week now, and still *nothing* had happened. And, she owned, apart from feeling edgy and restless, she was getting to be rather fed up with the situation.

Fed up with Grant Harrington and his brusque sarcastic tongue, too, she thought. Because although he seemed set on wrapping her in cotton wool; and there could be no other name for the way he insisted she didn't do a hand's turn in the house, he was making no secret that to possess her was still his aim—so why on earth didn't he do something about it!

It was a week ago today that he had introduced her to Mrs Podmore. A week since, deliberately going to his office later than usual so that he could instruct his daily—who although she appeared a very prim soul had softened rapidly from her askance look to find an unmarried lady in

residence—'Miss Johnston is convalescing here while her
father is away on business.' And after advising that she
was only recently out of hospital after major surgery, he
had instructed, 'Miss Johnston may want to give a hand in
the house, but I'd be obliged, Mrs Podmore, if you would
see to it that she rests as much as possible.'

'I can keep my own room tidy,' Devon, not liking any of
this, had butted in—only to receive an avuncular look
from Grant in Mrs Podmore's presence, and he had
patted her arm, and said:

'You know you're not up to making your own bed yet,
Devon dear.' And turning to Mrs Podmore who was
smiling now that it was clear that they were not sharing
the same bed, not seeing beneath the remark the intimation that soon, having metaphorically made her own bed,
Devon would be lying in his, he had commented, 'Miss
Johnston just isn't up to lifting and turning mattresses yet,
although she would deny it.'

Mrs Podmore had further proof that Grant's story
about her major surgery was true, when that evening, the
glorious spell of weather holding, he had brought home
a swimsuit he had purchased for Devon, handing it
to her with the instruction, 'Get some sun on you tomorrow.'

She had no intention of wearing anything he purchased
for her. But the next day had turned out to be a scorcher.
And stiffnecked though she could be at times, the heat
combined with common sense telling her the sun's healing
rays could do her scar tissue nothing but good, at eleven
she had changed into the swimsuit and had gone out to the
sun-lounger. Whereupon Mrs Podmore coming out to
bring her refreshment, had seen her scars and had called
her, 'You poor love.' From then on she had been waited on
as though it was only yesterday she had had her last
operation. And Devon's only satisfaction in this state of

affairs was that she made sure she made her own bed each morning before Mrs Podmore arrived.

Absently, she reached for the coffee the kindly daily had just brought her, her mind going to the root of what was really getting her down. Grant had taken her out to dinner a couple of times, though more often Mrs Podmore prepared something they just had to warm up for their evening meal. And yesterday, as he had the previous Sunday, he had taken her out for a drive, so she couldn't exactly say she was fed up with staying at home the whole time. But what was keeping her awake at nights was the growing anxiety, the growing fear, knowing as she did that Grant still wanted his retribution, was that with him sending her to her room every night, as yet making no move to have his retribution—time was going on. He could not keep her father in Scotland indefinitely, her father was too astute not to smell something fishy if he had done all he thought necessary in the way of a feasibility study, yet was told to stay there. And she just *had* to be back in her own home when her father returned.

Her hand jerked, making her hastily return her coffee cup to the table at the memory of Grant questioning her in one of their idle after-dinner conversations, about the statement she had once made that she would not dream of marrying anyone until she had that 'all clear' from her medical consultant. She had been adamant then as she had told him that though her fears of regression were getting fainter and fainter, she still needed that final clearance from Mr McAllen before she would consider thinking that she could truly be like other girls.

He had mocked her a little, she recalled, a king of the art, but she would not budge from that deep-seated conviction that no amount of mockery could shake—and he had begun to look thoughtful.

Devon knew panic again as she thought about his

thoughtful look. Had he decided then that, when he didn't care who she married so long as it wasn't him, still he would not take her until after she had paid her last visit to Mr McAllen?

Oh God, she thought, breaking out into a lather, her appointment was two weeks away! Lord knew how long after that it would take for Grant to tire of her. Suppose he didn't tire of her straight away—her father could come home—Oh God . . .

Panicking madly, wanting it all out of the way before her father returned, fresh panic started as she recalled that her parent had always attended every appointment with her. What if he took it into his head to make a flying visit home to go with her on her last appointment? Her thoughts latched on to only one fact—for her father's peace of mind, it had to be all over before he came home. And it had to be soon, for the sooner it started, the sooner it would all be at an end.

Mrs Podmore, coming out to collect her coffee cup, though leaving it when she could see she hadn't finished, made Devon try hard to hold down her panic.

'You've made your bed again,' tut-tutted the daily. 'You really shouldn't, Miss Johnston.'

Useless, she knew, to tell her that she felt fine. 'Force of habit,' she replied, dredging up a smile.

'You're looking pale—are you feeling all right?' asked Mrs Podmore, peering at her closely.

'Never better,' said Devon, getting up and leaving the lounger. 'In fact, I think I'll go and wash my hair.'

Having escaped Mrs Podmore, Devon could not escape her thoughts. Grant, for all his sarcasm, his mockery, was wrapping her in cotton wool and treating her like some convalescent. Countless were the times when she went to give him a hand with something, when he would tell her to go and sit down. And that, she was firmly convinced now, was because he didn't want a frustrating second attempt to make her his when the time came. It *had* to mean that he was waiting until Mr McAllen had told her she was as normal as any other girl.

Mrs Podmore departed at midday. During the afternoon the phone rang, but Devon did not answer it. She heard it, ignored it, and went back to her plan of action.

Grant arrived home around six, and Devon, with her newly washed hair and prettiest dress with, as if by accident, the top button of the vee neck undone, turned from the drinks cabinet ready to hand him the single measure of Scotch he liked as he walked through the sitting room door.

She smiled, her hand with the glass in it thrust forward. But the come-hither 'Hello, Grant' she had been practising never got uttered. For his face was as black as thunder as he looked from her shining hair—too much of a man not to notice that, lightly tanned, rested, and with a button tantalisingly undone at her bosom, she was quite something.

'Where the hell were you this afternoon?' he rapped without preamble. His ignoring the Scotch had her returning it to the tray as she swallowed down this setback to her plans, and wondered what had gone wrong with his day.

'I wasn't anywhere but here,' she replied.

'Then why didn't you answer the phone?'

'I didn't know it was you,' she said, calm starting to desert. And snappily, 'I have no wish to advertise that I'm here as your—house guest.' She bit her lip, knowing her manner was very far from what she wanted. 'Why did you ring?' she asked, forcing a smile, forcing a pleasantness she did not feel in the face of his dark look. 'Was it something important?'

'I'm going to change,' he said, and abruptly went,

leaving her knowing that when it came to seduction scenes, she was a rank amateur.

It was later, dinner almost over, that Devon, putting herself out to be pleasant and receiving monosyllabic answers for reward, knew that it just wasn't going to work. Oh, she had seen Grant's eyes on her more times than enough to know that he was aware of her. But even, when it would have been easier and far more natural for her to ask him to pass the out-of-reach cruet, she had leant across the table for it, thereby giving him full view of her cleavage, Grant had not risen with one of those remarks that would previously have been guaranteed to make her blush.

Frustrated herself in her efforts to get him to take the initiative, the meal was almost at an end when, realising she never was going to make headway in the unversed way she was attempting, Devon suddenly exploded, and asked him point blank.

'Tell me straight, Grant Harrington,' she said, her voice cold, her face showing now none of the pleasantness she had been at pains to show him, 'is it your intention to wait until I've seen Mr McAllen before you—we . . .' she was getting flustered, 'or what?' she ended lamely.

'Ah,' he drawled, making her wish she had something solid in her hands to hit him with as he leaned back in his chair and contemplated her mutinous face. 'You've been trying to tell me something ever since I got in, haven't you, Devon?'

He knew *exactly* what it was she had been trying, she thought, angered that he had let her carry on with her attempt, while all the time he had seen straight through it. Woodenly, she wouldn't give him the satisfaction of knowing he was right.

'Which is it, Devon?' he asked, his eyes flicking mockingly to her undone button and back to her face. 'Have you decided I'm not such a swine after all? Or is it that you're just plain hot to have your wicked way with me?'

She could do without the comedy. 'Neither,' she told him in no uncertain terms. And, since this was too important to her for prevarication, 'My clinic appointment is two weeks today, and . . .'

'I haven't forgotten,' he cut in, his voice cool, his tones even, when she was in danger of getting all stewed up.

'And neither will my father have forgotten,' she said bluntly, while knowing it might have been better if she kept her father out of this, but having been too worked up thinking about it that afternoon to leave him out of it now. 'He has always accompanied me on my appointments,' she went on, groaning inwardly as she saw that mention of her father had succeeded in making Grant look uptight. 'I can't—can't help but worry that he might take a few accumulated days off so as to come with me,' she made herself finish—and for her efforts, had the harsh retort:

'I had noticed his taking ways.'

He was back to being the hard man she had first known, and still was, she thought, restraining the impulse his remark about her father had wrought, of wanting to upend one of the tureens over his head. But having got this far, she had spent too anguished an afternoon to storm to her room as she wanted.

'If it's all the same to you,' she pushed on, never in her life having visualised having a conversation such as this one, 'I'd just as soon have—er—everything—out of the way before my father returns.'

'You really *are* trying to tell me something,' he replied, cool again, that mockery back.

'Damn you!' she shouted, her temper shot. 'If you still want me, then . . .'

'Oh, I still want you, Devon Johnston,' he broke in on her, his eyes going over her, a devil dancing in their dark depths suddenly at her flush of colour at his words. 'And—with regard to your visit to your physician—you really mustn't go around crediting me with virtues I just haven't got.'

Which had to mean, she thought, that he had no intention of waiting until she had seen Mr McAllen! But before she could question him further, he was making her go scarlet, by saying:

'Added to which, my dear Devon, I carry such a beautiful picture of you and your naked—charms— around with me, that I think I can be fairly certain that the month or so I sent your father away for is not going to be nearly enough for my desire for you to be quenched.'

If he had been trying to alarm her, then he had succeeded. All too evident was it that Grant had sent her father away on a phoney errand. But what concerned her more, was paramount, to her way of thinking, was that she had to try and get that desire quenched, and the sooner the better. Had she thought for an instant that Grant would change his mind about the retribution he wanted, then she would have tried that avenue, but, resigned now as she had become, it had to be *now*.

'That night,' she said, grabbing at all the calm she had left. 'That night when we . . .' Oh lord, this was terrible. 'I'd done too much—prior to that,' she said, swallowing hard and trying again. 'What with chasing around getting my father ready to go off,' she explained, inserting hastily, 'because he was so upset by—everything else, I didn't tell him about me having to rest.'

She knew she was babbling on, but she didn't seem able to stop—not with the nub of the whole matter looming large.

'Anyway,' she resumed, Grant sitting quietly watching, but this time not interrupting, 'I'd done too much. I know I shouldn't have lugged my cases from the bus stop, but . . .' She stopped when his face took on a tight-lipped expression again. 'Well, anyway,' she said, feeling all hot and clammy, 'I haven't felt even the smallest niggle in nearly a week now.'

'So . . . ?' he enquired, being obtuse on purpose, she was certain.

And that just about did it. Here she was going under at what she was trying to tell him, and when his brain was always about ten steps ahead of hers, here he was making out he didn't have an idea what she was talking about.

'Damn you!' she exploded, embarrassment flying in the face of provoked rage. 'What I'm trying to tell you is that since I'm not in any pain now, there's no need for you to sleep in that big bed alone.'

She was crimson-faced as those last words left her. And she was struggling desperately for control when Grant looked at her for long moments without speaking. And then he had her fighting with all she had not to physically lash out at him, when slowly he drawled:

'Now how about that for an invitation!'

Taking a mammoth breath for control, aware of his eyes on her heaving bosom, Devon stayed in there as though glued.

'But an invitation you're not going to take up tonight?' she questioned tautly.

For a moment, as she saw his eyes start to smoulder as they left their fascination with her rising and falling breasts, and returned to her face, Devon thought she had won. She even began to feel that thrill of a different panic as Grant rose from his chair, and looked as though he would come over to her.

But she was staggered when, expecting to feel his arms around her at any moment, she saw him half turn away, and heard his curt, 'Tonight my fancy is for a more experienced woman.' And as she stood and stared stupified, he strode across to the door, and had one last instruction for her. 'Leave the washing up—Mrs Podmore will see to it in the morning.'

Militantly, Devon slammed into the washing up. Damn him, damn him! she thought, unintentionally breaking a plate and not caring, hoping it was part of his best dinner service, damn his eyes!

Having gone to bed and lain there, positive she wasn't at all interested in what time he got back from his 'experienced woman', a picture of the stunning Vivien came to her and just would not leave. Damn him, she thought again—and was certain it was not pique that she felt. He could take himself off with a dozen Viviens and she still wouldn't care.

Again Devon had a wakeful night, but it was not until halfway through the next morning that it came to her, impossible though it seemed, that it had not been worry over her father's peace of mind that had kept her awake this time!

By midday of the following Monday, she had just about had it with Grant Harrington's vow of celibacy—where she was concerned—Mrs Podmore's fussing, and The Limes convalescent home in general.

Last Monday had not been the only evening Grant had gone out. She had tried again on Thursday to get through to him, and again he had gone out. No wonder he wasn't champing at the bit to get *her* into bed with him, she thought sourly.

For a further ten minutes Devon railed against Grant Harrington and the fact that she would not feel her father secure until she had let that swine of a man have *his* wicked way with her. Then, moved by a spirit that said 'Who did he think he was?' and recalling clearly that he had not liked it that day she hadn't answered the telephone and he had thought she had gone out, she waited only until Mrs

Podmore had gone for the day—then she too left The Limes.

She let herself into her own home, delighted to see that her father had managed to find time to drop her a note. He was well, he said, but was busy. Reading between the lines, she guessed he would work himself to a standstill to do a good job to prove to Grant that he would not let him down a second time. She would write him a chatty letter back, she thought, seeing that his scribbled communication must have lain on the hall carpet for a week now, according to the postmark. He would only start to fret if he didn't hear from her soon.

Her feelings of defiance against Grant Harrington had been weakened by a few hours in the sanctuary of her own home. But at five, and because she had no alternative, Devon went to catch a bus back to The Limes. And having swung round from being ready to look for a fight with him, luckier with public transport than she had been before, in a much less contentious frame of mind, she made it to the foot of the drive with about fifteen minutes to spare before he usually came home.

To see his car parked outside the front door was enough to tell her that today he had broken from routine. Anticipating trouble, her chin tilted—she wasn't a prisoner, for goodness' sake, she thought, but she knew that was exactly what she was. A prisoner to the dictates of the man who would surely have her father incarcerated in a prison with bars, if she did not jump when he said 'jump'.

His glowering expression when she went in said it all. 'I didn't expect you home yet,' she heard herself get in first. Then she realised she was sounding guilty, and came quickly off the defensive. 'I went home—to see if there was any mail,' she tacked on, hating that her offensive had soon crumpled in the face of his furious look, and that she had quickly invented an excuse.

'You went by taxi, of course?' he asked shortly.

'It didn't occur to me to . . .'

'You took a bus—you walked to and from the bus stop! That's a good half mile, plus the distance the other end.'

To Devon it seemed that he was more concerned that she had walked anywhere than he was that she hadn't been there when he had got in. And she was just about fed up with the way she, in her view, was being over-protected.

'Exercise is good for me,' she snapped in a spurt of temper.

'I'll remember that,' he said, fire lighting his eyes as he took in the blue flame in hers. But she noted, for all that fire, he made no move to come anywhere near her. Though he did manage to confuse her when he held out his hand, palm uppermost, and said, 'Keys.'

'Keys?' she questioned, her brow wrinkling.

'The keys to your house. I'll collect any mail that arrives for you.'

Devon was back to thinking Swine, swine, swine! when she went to bed that night. Of course she'd had to hand over her keys, he'd been adamant about that. Though she did have a small victory in that she knew exactly under which plant pot in the garden shed a spare key to the front door was hidden.

Nursing her small feeling of triumph the next day, Devon felt less mutinous when she got up. But when Grant arrived home a little later than usual that night, and handed her a picture postcard from her father, then told her that her father had chanced to telephone while he was there, she was back to wanting to take a sledge-hammer to him.

'You *answered* the phone!' she squeaked. And rapidly, 'What did he say? What did you tell him?' Vivid pictures of her father's peace of mind going up in smoke beset her.

And it didn't help one iota that Grant was calm where she was threatening to blow a fuse, as he chose to answer her second question.

'I told him I was taking you out to dinner, and that you were upstairs getting ready.'

'What—did he say?' she asked, her first rush of panic on the wane.

'He said that he'd phoned a couple of times and that you must have been out,' Grant replied evenly. And, a devil lighting his eyes so she just knew she wasn't going to like what was coming, he added, 'I told him we were seeing a lot of each other, but that I hoped—to see a lot more of you.'

'That's not funny,' she retorted acidly, and could have hit him when all she had for a reply was an infuriating grin. 'What did he say to that?' she asked him freezingly.

'What you'd expect,' he said. 'Came on the heavy parent, forgot I was his employer, and told me you weren't like other girls.' He paused, then had her staring at him wide-eyed when he revealed, 'I told him I knew all about your surgery.'

'But not,' she swallowed, 'but not that you knew why he had—stolen from you?'

His grin disappeared, and if she had tried to freeze him, his voice was hard and like ice when he rapped back, 'The money wasn't discussed.' Flattened, she saw his expression change again, even if he was carelessly studying the headlines in the evening paper draped over the back of the settee, as he said, 'Though he did seem to think, since you must have told me the dark secret of your operation, that you must think quite something of me.'

She wasn't that flattened. And when Grant had raised his eyes to look at her, as lofty as he occasionally was, she tossed at him:

'What quaint ideas parents sometimes get!'

And he had bounced back, not entirely unexpectedly, 'Don't they, though—I'm sure he thinks my intentions are honourable.'

That night Devon wrote a long and happy-sounding letter to her parent. And because, in the light of Grant's telephone conversation with him, he would suspect something was wrong if she didn't mention it, she told him how she had gone out with his employer a couple of times, and how she had enjoyed it.

But having sealed her letter and got into bed, disturbed by the thought that she hated lying to her parent, Devon was brought up short to realise that she had not lied to him. She had been out with Grant a couple of times, and she had, when she thought about it—enjoyed those outings! She pulled the covers over her head and tried to sleep. She was, she thought, to say the least, feeling not a little confused.

Confusion was to be hers too the following morning, when while it was still very early, something wakened her. Confusion and heart-bumping panic were immediately mingled. For, her eyes going enormous, she discovered that Grant was in her room!

For that moment, as her throat dried and she realised that he had chosen *now* as the time to claim his retribution, she was too stunned to take in that he was dressed and didn't look likely to tell her to make some room for him in her single bed.

'Don't panic,' he instructed, watching her saucer eyes and not having too much bother in reading her thoughts. 'I have to go away for a few days—I thought you might want to kiss me goodbye.'

Panic fled as she took in his business suit, but confusion stayed. Somehow it didn't seem right that he wouldn't be coming home tonight.

'With pleasure,' she replied, doing her best with sarcasm that early in the morning.

She struggled to sit up, then found she need not have bothered. For Grant had parked himself on the edge of her bed, and had taken hold of her. And as he covered her mouth with his own, and his body came into close contact, so as his kiss deepened and her hands came to his shoulders, she found she was being pressed back against the mattress.

She was sure afterwards that she had not clung to him, but his lingering kiss did disturb her—she had to admit that. But suddenly Grant was breaking away, taking her hands from his shoulders and pushing them back to her.

Then he was moving quickly to the door as though he was running late. Though he did have time to spare for one last look at her as she lay with her tousled silky blonde hair against her pillows. And he did have time for one last taunting comment.

'Try not to miss me too much,' he mocked. Then, very definitely serious, 'And make sure you're still here when I get back on Friday.'

CHAPTER NINE

HAVING risen early that Wednesday that Grant went away, Devon was out of the house to post her letter before Mrs Podmore arrived. Though the daily was there when she got back, and was sympathetic when she told her that Mr Harrington had gone away on business.

'He often does,' replied Mrs Podmore. 'What a shame he had to go while you're here, though. You'll feel lonely in this big house by yourself, I expect.'

She hadn't been at all lonely, Devon told herself when she went to bed that night. Though it wouldn't have hurt him to put a three-minute telephone call through—even if he did know she wouldn't answer the phone. It did not occur to her that she might be thinking a shade illogically!

Thursday seemed to be a day that went on for ever. The phone stayed quiet, the house was quiet, and it was no wonder, she thought, that she should be fed up. And as she remembered the first half of Grant's departing shot, it certainly was not that she was missing him, that she felt so out of sorts.

She had not slept well the previous night, but as she tried to settle down to sleep that night, a thousand and one thoughts visited her, so that in actual fact, on Thursday night, she barely slept at all.

She knew full well why Grant couldn't put himself out to pick up the phone, of course. But that her imagination should provide her with vivid pictures of some stunning, *experienced* female, she could do without. What did she care whom he was out with? Or who it was who kept him so fully occupied that he had forgotten completely that he had a less experienced female established in his home? A female whom, she thought, anger stimulating her into further sleeplessness, he had told, 'Be here when I get back.'

Like hell she'd be there when he got back! she fumed—and was then visited by a whole jumble of thoughts that further prevented sleep. How could she leave? There was her father to think of! And oh, lord, her appointment with Mr McAllen was on Monday—it would look well if, as she had thought before, her father decided to make a quick visit to go with her!

Two minutes after she had dropped off into an exhausted sleep, or that was the way it seemed, Devon opened her eyes and saw it was time to get up. She could have lain there a few more hours catching up on the night's sleep she had missed, but the thought of Mrs Podmore had her dragging herself wearily out of bed. Mrs Podmore was sure to think she was ill if she hadn't surfaced when she arrived, and the thought of her fussing over her was more than she could take that morning.

But however little sleep she had managed to get in, thoughts that had kept her awake were still with her as she bathed and dressed and went downstairs.

'Good morning, Mrs Podmore,' she greeted brightly, when on the stroke of nine she arrived.

'Good morning, Miss Johnston,' Mrs Podmore replied, looking at her closely before she set down her basket and changed into her 'comfy' shoes. 'You look a little peaky this morning. Are you all right?'

Feeling she must have bags under her eyes down to her knees, Devon kept a bright smile. 'I'm fine,' she said. 'Fine.' And, ready to say anything to head her off, for she could see Mrs Podmore was about to suggest she went and sat down while she made her a nice cup of tea, off the top of her head she said, 'Mr Harrington comes back today.'

Mrs Podmore smiled. 'I expect you'll be looking forward to that.' And, still smiling, 'Though I daresay Mr Harrington has phoned each evening to see if you're all right?'

See, Devon thought, as she smiled as if to convey that Grant had never been off the phone, even Mrs Podmore thought it was natural he should exert himself to pick up the phone. Well, if he couldn't be bothered to ring, then he could go and whistle! By the very fact that he had commanded her to hand over the keys to her home, she knew he did not want her going there. Well, tough luck, she thought. Besides which, if as she suspected, her father might take it into his head to come home—and God knew what she was going to do about that—then she was just not going to let him come home to a place that looked as though it had not been lived in.

Prefixing her statement with a phrase she was getting tired of trotting out, 'The doctor said exercise is good for me,' Devon allayed Mrs Podmore's fears, then told her, 'I thought I'd go for a walk this morning.' And, knowing she wouldn't be back before twelve, 'Though of course I shall hail a taxi if I feel in the least tired,' adding, 'I think I may stay in town for lunch.'

Half past ten saw her in the garden shed of her home, satisfaction hers as her fingers took up the spare key to the front door.

Mentally thumbing her nose at Grant Harrington, she was soon in the house and had all the windows open before she got down to work. First she made a fruit cake, then pastry, then she cleaned up the kitchen before she collected up the brass from every room, and then set about giving it a good polish.

There were few fresh supplies in the house, and even though hoping she was mistaken and that this weekend would see neither hide nor hair of her father, she just could not bear that he should return home without so much as a crust of bread in the house.

Shopping took longer than she had thought. And it was four o'clock before she had everything put away and had decided she would have something to eat. A bowl of soup and some toast, plus a jam tart made from left-over pastry, sent hunger pangs away.

Once more Devon cleaned up the kitchen, making a mental note to put the fruit cake in a tin just before she left. It should be cold by then. Just time then to flick a quick duster round the place, she thought, and while she was upstairs she had better close the windows.

It was peculiar, she thought, as she went downstairs again, a duster pushed into the pocket of her overall as the need came to her to take her ease on the settee for a moment, that one never realised how tired one was until one sat down.

Of course, she had barely slept last night. And she had rather used up her spare energy on rushing about a bit today. But, in a glorious feeling of elation she had not felt since that day she had come back from Sweden, she had hared around the shops, been up and down stairs numerous times today, and oh, how marvellous!—understandably weary as she felt, not so much as the tiniest niggle did she feel in her hip!

It was ages since she had stretched out on the settee, she thought, and for the pure experience of doing so when there was absolutely no need, she raised her feet from the floor, a smile picking up the corners of her mouth as she made herself comfortable—and closed her eyes.

It had been broad daylight when she had sat down on the settee, she remembered, when something startled her awake and she opened her eyes. But it was not daylight now, and as she blinked and her eyes adjusted to electric light, she gaped to see, more furious than she had ever seen him, Grant Harrington standing with his hand still on the light switch.

Realising it had been the light coming on that had startled her awake, and that when she had meant to be back at The Limes when he returned, she must have fallen asleep, and been asleep for hours, trying not to get alarmed that he looked ready to throttle her as his hand fell from the light switch and he approached, she asked:

'What—time is it?'

'Time you learned some bloody sense!' was her not very forthcoming answer.

Then long arms were stretching down to haul her to her feet. And, not waiting for her to do it herself, he began unbuttoning the overall she still had on, the tell-tale duster hanging from its pocket revealing what she had been up to.

'Get your shoes on,' he ordered, stripping the overall from her.

Devon obeyed his grunted instruction, but was coming more and more awake by the minute. Obviously he had just got home and, weary himself, was as mad as hell that he had had to turn out again to come looking for her.

'Business satisfactory?' she dared to enquire—and finding her annoyance with him rearing again that he had not telephoned yet expected her to stay put, 'Or are you late because of *other* business?'

For a moment she thought he was going to flatten her with one of his short and sharp replies. Then a look appeared in his eyes she couldn't fathom, and he was biting down whatever it had been he was going to flatten her with, though he succeeded in flattening her neverthe-less, when he said shortly:

'I'm not in a mood to pay any attention to your jealous little barbs. It's nearly eleven. Get going.'

'*Jealous!*' He would have edged her out of the door, but

his accusation had her standing her ground. 'My God, you *have* been overworking!' she flared—and found his patience, never very dense, had suddenly worn thin.

'*Move*,' he roared, 'or I'll damn well carry you!'

Devon jumped at his tone, and moved quickly out into the hall. But there a sudden recollection came to her, and she turned left, not right. 'I made a cake,' she muttered, and went scooting off to the kitchen.

With Grant getting madder and madder she put the cake away in a tin and heard him snarl, 'It's no wonder you were spark out when I came in,' and accusing, 'You've been on your feet all day!'

'I'm not an invalid,' she flared.

But she had time only to put the lid on the cake tin, the tin having to be left out on the kitchen table. For at that point, Grant Harrington quietly blew his top.

As though she weighed nothing at all, in the next moment he grabbed her up, and flicking lights off as he went, an ominous quietness showing in the deliberate way he moved, he carried her outside. He did not set her down when they reached his car, but opened the passenger door and, not saying another word, placed her in the front seat—and all at once Devon was scared.

The drive back to The Limes was completed without one syllable being uttered, and Devon was fast growing of the opinion that the sooner she took herself off to bed, the better for her it would be. Perhaps by the morning, when he had recovered his temper, she would be able to tell him that she had not done so very much that day. Perhaps after a decent night's sleep she wouldn't be feeling so frayed around the edges either.

That same ominous quietness was still about him when they reached his home. Devon did not wait for him to come round to let her out, not looking forward to, if she didn't move quickly enough a second time, being picked up and thrown indoors.

She was up the steps and had the key he had given her inside the lock before he had joined her. He flicked on the hall light as they went in, and thinking it would be far better if she said nothing, when anything she said, what with her feeling on edge and his mammoth temper looking for a spark, all hell could be let loose, her eyes went to the stairs.

She had actually taken two steps towards those stairs when Grant's voice, quiet behind her, asked:

'Have you eaten today?'

She so very nearly flared then that, as mad as he was with her, he was still into looking after her welfare.

'Yes,' she replied stiffly, adding a tight, 'thank you,' because that was the way she had been brought up. 'I'll say goodnight,' she found herself tacking on, 'I'm going to bed.'

She had made it to the bottom of the stairs this time, when his voice, from exactly the same spot, telling her that he had not moved, came again. 'Devon.' She didn't like the way he said her name, it sounded—threatening! But she halted. Then because he had something else to add, and didn't look like addressing it to her back, she turned to face him.

He had that quiet look to him still, she saw. But he looked too like a man who had more than one ace up his sleeve. And suddenly, when she already knew that he was capable of repaying outstanding debts without the use of money, Devon knew fear.

She was right to know fear, she soon learned. For, his voice more cool than quiet, he succeeded monument-ally in freezing on the instant any flicker of a hot edgy reply when, his eyes watchful for reaction, he dropped out:

'*A propos* you not being an invalid, make it the—big bed.'

The silky smile that answered her wide-eyed, shattered look was all she needed to know that he meant it! And while she knew that she should be glad, glad, glad, that something was going to happen, that a start was being made to free her father from the fate that awaited him, she turned away from Grant Harrington, her intelligence telling her something else as well.

She washed and changed into her night things in the room she had always used, barring that one night. She knew now why Grant was so furious with her. It wasn't just that she had disobeyed him and had not been there when he had got back. All too clearly she knew then, as admitting to nerves, she left her room and went to the room that housed the big bed, was the fact that having seen to it that she rested, having not taken her during those early weeks which he must have thought of as a convalescent period for her, he had been building up to get her fit so that the debt she had incurred through her father should be discharged.

Grant had not wanted to be put off again by any moan of pain she uttered. But clearly, tonight, whether she moaned from pain or not would be immaterial to him. He was so angry with her for wearying herself with housework and baking—having no idea that she had fallen asleep on the settee more because she had barely slept a wink last night than through her exertions of the day—that tonight he was mad enough to make her his without thought or regard for her old injury.

Telling herself she had to be glad that this moment had arrived was of no help at all to quieten the butterflies she was experiencing as she shed her robe and climbed into the big bed.

As before, she put out the bedside lamp and plunged the

room into darkness. And as before she prayed, but with little hope, that angry as he was, he would not be rough with her. And, as before, she waited.

An age seemed to pass before the opening of the bedroom door had her heart thundering against her rib cage. Again Grant did not put on the light, but moved quietly around in the darkness. Then he was beside her in the big bed, and was lying on his back, but as far as she could tell, a mile away, for he was not touching her.

Expecting at any moment that he would reach for her, Devon lay rigid. Then she heard, anger seeming to be gone from him, she thought, the quiet question:

'Are you awake?'

For one crazily pitched moment it came to her to wonder—would he, if she did not answer, think she was asleep and not disturb her? She discounted that as that crazy thought was followed by. What choice had she but to answer? Her father could return at any time.

'Y-yes,' she replied, her voice husky, a trembling beginning in her that now, now he would take her in his arms.

The bedcovers heaved as he moved. And Devon, her heart drumming, was suddenly staggered to hear Grant say, 'Then go to sleep.' And as the bedclothes settled again, she was stupefied to find he had—turned his back on her!

Hardly believing it, her thoughts went off at a tangent. He was playing with her! He didn't mean it! What was she doing in his bed if it wasn't . . . Had he gone off the idea? Had he gone off the idea altogether? Her father . . .

The sound of even breathing coming from the other side of the bed told her that Grant had not been playing with her. He must have been overworking and had tired himself out! Hard on the heels of that thought came another that said he had tired himself out, but not from overwork. That he had satiated his appetite for a woman elsewhere made her feel angry. How dared he? she thought, and was furious with him, a sick feeling coming to her until she remembered his remark about her being jealous.

Rot, she thought, knowing perfectly well that she wasn't in the least jealous. It was only because that threat still hung over her father that she was getting so stewed up.

Her thoughts then began to grow bitty, and as her eyes closed, so her thoughts became half sentences. The bed was warm, and comfortable, and in another few minutes she was forgetting that she did not have the bed to herself.

As dawn filtered through the window, Devon moved in her sleep and came into contact with a naked and warm manly chest. Unused to bumping into anything in her solitary bed, she was instantly awake, her hand snatching back at so personal a contact.

Though, oddly, she felt neither shock nor surprise to find that Grant no longer had his back to her, but had moved during the night and was now sleeping with an arm wrapped around her shoulders, and that her head was very near to his head.

Too soon awake to wonder why that arm should feel so comfortable, she wondered instead, was Grant awake too? His breathing was even, so he must be asleep, she thought, and without further thought, she had moved her head so she could look at him.

The shock she would have thought natural a second or two earlier visited her the instant she saw his sleeping expression. But it was not that even in sleep his mouth still had that firm look to it that was the cause of her shock. Or that with his eyes closed he looked strangely contented to have her in his arms—which was ridiculous, she had to own later, for since she had not felt him gather her to him, he most likely had not consciously taken hold of her. But

what shocked her, and caused her to make a small in-
voluntary movement as though an electric charge had
unexpectedly gone through her, was that suddenly, blind-
ingly, in that moment, she knew that—she was in love
with him!

She flicked her eyes away from his face, not believing it.
It couldn't be true! Why, only last night she had been near
to hating him! Her eyes went back to him again, and she
was visited by such a feeling of tenderness for him, she just
had to know that it was true. That she, Devon Johnston,
was in love, with Grant Harrington.

That feeling of overwhelming tenderness took over.
Quietly she moved her head forward, and gently, no
longer in charge of herself, she softly laid her lips over the
shoulder nearest to her.

I love him, she thought, and with no thought then in her
head that Grant did not love her, a peace came over her.
She felt safe, secure in his arms—and she loved him. And
loving him, knowing he had been dead beat last night and
was not likely to wake up for a few more hours, she could
just not resist the urge to kiss him, just once more.

Only this time when she laid her mouth over the
warmth of him, his shoulder moved. Quickly she pulled
back. But even as she moved, the arm about her tightened.
And Devon knew as her eyes shot to his face and she saw
that dark eyes were open and were fastened on her, that it
was the feel of her lips on him that had awakened him.

'I—didn't mean to—wake you,' she said, it seeming out
of place in that moment to talk above a whisper, even as
she thought it would have been far better for him to think
she had slipped towards him in her sleep.

'I'd like to be woken every morning in that same way,'
he said softly back. And he smiled so that she just did not
see then that he was not referring to her in particular, and
that any woman kissing him awake would fit the bill.

Her love for him had her smiling back, no thought in her head to move away. She loved him, and never had she felt this close to him.

It seemed natural that he should raise his head from his pillow to kiss her. And just as natural that, his movements unhurried, he should slowly move her until she was on her back, his chest over hers as, gently, he kissed her again.

There was a smile in his eyes when he pulled back from her. 'You're beautiful,' he whispered, and kissed her eyes, drawing away to tell her, 'Your eyes are beautiful.' Then kissing her gently again, he told her, 'Everything about you is beautiful.'

The next time he kissed her, Devon's arms went up and around him. And as his kiss lengthened and deepened, there was no thought whatsoever in her head, her heart full and all for Grant, of her father. She loved Grant, she loved him.

What was showing in her eyes she neither knew nor cared. But when again Grant looked at her, then drew a sharp breath, then as his head came down and he kissed her again, and breathed, 'My darling,' Devon just did not want to let him go.

Her arms held him to her, and again he was looking into her eyes, at her love-pink skin, at the tenderness in her for him that she had never shown him before.

'I want you,' he said, his voice husky in his throat. And as a gentle kiss fluttered to the side of her mouth, 'Do you want me, Devon?'

Her answer was to place a hand in his hair, to pull his head that short distance needed. And, her lips parting, she kissed him.

His hands caressing her, his kisses embracing her, Devon's colour warmed. She returned kiss for kiss as her breasts were moulded, kissed, and tormented. A screaming need for him was being drawn from her as, not hurrying, he took her to a higher pitch.

And then, suddenly, it was all over—so suddenly that she was in small shock again. She had moaned in pure and utter rapture at what his touch was doing to her. And it was that moan of pleasure that had all ease from the fierce wanting he had wreaked in her snatched from her grasp.

Bewildered that, as though he had been scalded, Grant shot from the bed, she heard him swear, heard a sound like that of utterly unbearable frustration. And while the flush from his lovemaking was still glowing on her cheeks, she saw, not believing it, that without turning her way once, Grant had somehow got a robe around him, and with hurricane speed, and quite as devastating, he had left her.

Stunned, she had not the least chance of shrugging her shoulders and going back to sleep. Indeed, five minutes later, her love-drugged brain starting to clear, she was still sitting gaping at the door Grant had so rapidly exited through.

But her brain *was* clearing. And because she needed to find an answer to why had he bolted when it had looked as though there was not the smallest chance of that, Devon came out from her delirium to think that either her moan of ecstasy had triggered off reminders for him of that moan of pain he had wrought in her before—memories that as yet she had not been declared fully fit by her doctor—or that he had suddenly realised that to be giving herself so freely must mean that she loved him!

Hot colour of embarrassment rioted through her. She felt despair all at once that like a fool she had fallen in love with him. And nightmare anguish was vying for precedence, that her love was unwanted by him, and that he had no intention of getting ensnared with some female who, from the very way she had been, looked as though she might want to cling on long after he had tired of her.

It was then that thoughts of her father began to intrude. And once they had intruded, Devon was to be overwhelmed with anxiety again. For, whatever reason Grant had for going off the idea of wanting to make love to her, gone off the idea he very definitely had—so where did that leave her father?

An hour later, bathed, dressed, and hoping she looked more composed than she felt, Devon thought she had screwed up sufficient courage to go downstairs and face Grant Harrington.

He was clean-shaven and was dressed as, her expression wooden, she went into the sitting room where he was. She saw his face too was set in solemn lines, which had her sending further stiffening to her spine as she fought to eject the image of his smiling eyes, his mouth turned up at the corners, just before he had kissed her.

'I . . .' she started coldly—and got severely chopped off before she could utter another syllable.

'Get packed,' he ordered, gravel in his voice.

'Packed?' she exclaimed, fear, apprehension for her father mingling with deep despair that Grant had no use for her love, as she fought with all she had so he should know that any idea he had that she loved him in any small degree was a figment of his imagination.

'I'm taking you back to your home,' he elucidated shortly.

'But . . .' it was killing her, but she had to stay in there, for her father's sake she had to bite down the 'Don't bother driving me, I'll find my own transport' 'But I—we . . .' Oh God, this was terrible. 'We haven't . . .' Devon found she could not follow that line further. But stubbornness was cementing her feet to the floor. 'What about my father?' she asked bluntly, her voice waspish, which had him glowering at her for her trouble.

'Are you going to get packed, or do I do it for you?' he asked brusquely.

Never had she known she could be so stubborn. But his ignoring that very important question she had put had her ready to stay with her feet firmly planted on his carpet all day if need be.

'You can't prosecute him,' she challenged, no matter how firm her feet were, her legs feeling like water that he threw her a look that clearly told her not to tell him what to do. 'I came here fully prepared to—to do as you asked,' she made herself go on. And, about to go under for the third time, 'I still—am,' she forced through lips that objected to that admission.

Carelessly, Grant shrugged as he turned from her, his words cutting into her like acid as he tossed at her, 'Had you more experience,' and she was sure there was derision there, 'then you would know that there's nothing more guaranteed to turn a man off than to have a woman throw herself at him.'

Searing colour scorched her cheeks, so that she was glad he now had his back to her and could not witness it. And then, loving him even as she thought, you swine! Devon was glad that fury winged in that he could speak to her so. Though her words, when she did find them, were controlled and icy, as she said:

'I came here fully prepared to complete my half of the bargain we made. You cannot now,' she told him, grimly holding back on the fury that had erupted in her, 'go back on your word not to prosecute him.'

That he was still taking exception to her telling him what he could and could not do was evident by the sharp way he spun round, then threw at her roughly:

'I shall do whatever suits me!'

Her throat went dry at the threat behind his words. But if he had scorned her, then there was a whole world of scorning for him, as she retorted, 'Behind his back? While he's away in Scotland at . . .'

'I've already been on the phone,' he snarled, fury coming to him too that she was daring to jibe. 'Arrangements have been made for your father to fly home today.'

The wind was well and truly knocked out of her sails, and she stared at him thunderstruck. 'You've . . . He's . . .' she spluttered, all manner of fears striking. And never more had she wanted to poleaxe Grant Harrington when, his fury departing to see he had knocked the legs from under her, he drawled loftily:

'Now will you go and get packed?'

CHAPTER TEN

DEVON awoke in her own bedroom on Sunday. Her father had arrived home the previous night looking fit and well, and more than ready to tease her about her dates with Grant.

She got up and, dressed, went downstairs hoping, although he was such a dear, that her father would not resume his teasing this morning. Though even as she thought it, she saw that if she had had to wait so long to be just like any other girl, he had had a long wait too before he could treat her as such, teasing from one's parent being a natural part of family life.

The first one up—her father was having a lie-in after his journey—Devon went to the kitchen, her face pensive as she thought of the threat to his liberty that, though he did not know it, still hung over him. He had said last night that he had no idea why Grant had recalled him, but that if he had not yet come to a decision about whether or not he should return to his office come Monday, then he had brought enough paperwork back with him to last him through all of next week at home.

'Though,' he had added, his eyes twinkling as he began to tease again,' I shouldn't be at all surprised if Grant doesn't get in touch with *one* of us before Monday!'

She had coloured then, and had turned away, concern and love choking her that, seeing her through a father's eyes, he should think it unlikely that any man, having taken her out a couple of times, should not want to do so again. And while she knew that she ought to try to prepare him for that dreadful fate that would be his, there were

just no words in her then to tell him that because she had
been too forward, Grant had gone off her and that she had
lost not only all chance of ever seeing him again, but that
she had also lost him that chance of not seeing the inside of
a prison.

'I overslept,' said Charles Johnston, coming cheerfully
into the kitchen. 'A quick breakfast, I think, then I'll set
up office in the dining room. Can we eat lunch in the
kitchen, do you think?'

'I wouldn't dream of disturbing your paperwork,'
Devon agreed, and smiled, wanting to tell him he was
wasting his time doing paperwork that wouldn't be
needed—but she found she just could not.

Her father surfaced for lunch, a more lengthy meal than
breakfast had been, during the course of which Devon was
to find, ever with an eye to her care, that he was more
observant than he had been over his rushed breakfast.

'Something troubling you, Devon?' he asked, his face
serious, when she was clearing away the main course, her
plate barely touched.

With this opportunity to tell him, she looked at his dear
face, his hair prematurely white, and she just had to let
him be happy for a little while longer. 'No, not a thing,'
she replied, putting on a bright face—but only to find that
her parent knew her better than that. Though his specula-
tions were a mile off.

'Grant will be in touch, I'm sure he will,' he told her
gently, when she knew darn well the only communication
they would get from Grant would be through his solicitor.
Then, 'Ah-h,' he said, as if suddenly catching on, 'it's not
Grant, is it? It's your appointment with Mr McAllen
tomorrow. You always did get yourself keyed up just
before a visit to him.'

When he left the kitchen to return to his labours, Devon
was again choked. She had had to let him think that her

appointment with the consultant tomorrow afternoon was the only cloud on her horizon. She had been near to tears as he'd tried to get her out of her quiet mood by referring to what she had told him. 'Dr Henekssen said your last operation was a great success, didn't he?' he had coaxed. And she had smiled and had wanted to put her arms around him, for it just wasn't fair. He had done wrong, yes, but not for himself, never did he think of himself.

It was early evening when the door bell went. Her father had returned to his work in the dining room after emerging for a quick cup of tea and a sandwich, so Devon guessed as she went to answer the door that he would be too engrossed in what he was doing to want to disturb himself.

Remembering his surmise that Grant would be in touch, even if she didn't believe it, Devon could not help that her heart started to race overtime. But when she pulled back the door and saw that it was Grant standing there, dressed casually, and looking so aloof to see her again after his drawled 'there's nothing more guaranteed to turn a man off than to have a woman throw herself at him' she found she had invited him in without thinking, needing to turn her back on him for a few seconds as scarlet colour darted to her face.

It was Grant who closed the door, and Grant who spoke first, as for the moment she couldn't find anything to say to him.

'I've called to see your father,' he said coolly, and her fears for her father had her spinning round to look into his arrogant face. 'Privately,' he added succinctly.

'What do you want to see him about?' she asked sharply, loving him, yet wanting to hit him that he looked down his nose as though to say, that's my business. 'If you're going to upset him, I want to be in on it too,' she said heatedly, ignoring that Grant did not look well pleased.

'Upset him?' he said shortly, an angry look coming to him. 'Don't you yet know me better than that? Good God, woman, we've lived together . . .'

'Shut up!' she hissed, not missing his look of astonishment. 'I don't want my father to . . .'

The sound of the dining room door opening made her rapidly break off. Then her father was coming out into the hall, his hand outstretched as he said, 'I thought I heard your voice, Grant,' shaking hands with the big man, and consequently making relief wash over Devon, for having heard his voice, her father would never have shaken hands with Grant if he had heard what he had said.

'How's the job going?' queried her father's employer, his tone very different from the short way he had been with her.

'I'm working on it now.'

'I'll have a look, if I may,' said Grant. And as the two men strolled the few paces to the dining room, Devon ignored as she trailed behind them, they disappeared inside, where Grant turned and promptly shut the door on her.

Swine, pig! she thought, wandering back into the sitting room, but keeping the door open as she broke out into a sweat. One half of her wanted to barge in and make Grant Harrington say whatever he had to say in front of her, the other half remembered his 'Don't you yet know me better than that'. And the thought occurred, could she live with, laugh with, and love—leaving aside the times she had wanted to bash his head in—a man who would ultimately deprive her father of his freedom?

There had to be a certain something in Grant that was not harsh, aggressive and hard, for love in her to be born for him, she thought. And she was recalling his gentle lovemaking. But it wasn't only that. He was witty, sarcastic, but he was kind too. He had thought to get her a swimsuit so she could get the sun on her limbs. He had been considerate too. Though that didn't begin to analyse why she loved him—though she was afraid to think that yes, she did know him better than that because twice in the past she had thought he had let her off, and subsequently her father, but only to find that it was not so.

To Devon, waiting for the dining room to open, it seemed to be an hour before she heard the click of the door handle. And she was out in the hall like a streak of lightning, face to face with Grant as he emerged, then closed the door.

'Been listening at the keyhole, Devon?' he asked, one eyebrow arched, receiving his answer by the way she ignored his sarcasm and hissed:

'What have you said to him?' And without waiting for his reply, she tried to brush past him. 'I must go to him.'

A firm irremovable hand on her arm stopped her from going forward. But Grant had propelled her with him to the front door, and was standing looking down into her hostile face, before he did make any reply. And then it was clear he had no intention of telling her any of what had been said, when, his voice conversational almost, he asked:

'Is it tomorrow you go to see your consultant?'

He was the *limit*! Devon decided, battling hard to keep the lid on her fury that he was holding her there by force when what she wanted to do was to rush in to see her father.

'Don't tell me you've forgotten,' she snapped with hot sarcasm.

'What time is your appointment?'

Quietly seething, Devon saw the sooner she answered his questions, the sooner he would let go of her. 'Four o'clock,' she said tautly—and was little short of amazed when after considering her answer, he slowly drawled:

'There's a chance I may be free just before then. I'll give you a lift.'

'You'll give me . . .' Flabbergasted, she stared. Then, recovering, she was quick to tell him in no uncertain terms, 'I want nothing from you, Grant Harrington!'

But by now she was getting to know that look that said she was not going to like what was coming. As usual, he did not disappoint her.

'It didn't seem that way to me in the early hours of yesterday morning,' he softly let fall.

'You swine!' she hurled at him, but for all that, she went scarlet.

'When you look like that,' Grant drawled, a devil in his eyes as he observed her going all shades of pink, 'I'm sorely inclined to forget my—er—principles.'

She'd seen *that* look before too, that look, when the devil left his eyes, that said that whether her eagerness had put him off or no, right at this moment his need to possess her had returned. But he had already flattened her father with what he had told him, she was convinced of that. And so it was stiffly, borrowing some of his plentiful supply of arrogance, that she told him coldly:

'My father will take me to keep my appointment.' And because she could not help it, bitterly she threw at him, 'He'll be upset enough when you've done, without my taking the pleasure away of accompanying me on my last appointment.' Grant's enquiring eyebrow going skywards had her adding, 'My father has been looking forward to my final visit almost as much as I have.'

Her arm was suddenly free. 'Far be it from me to deprive him of anything,' he said, and turned to open the front door.

And Devon knew then, as she closed the door after him,

that that must be Grant at his satirical sarcastic best, for far from not wanting to deprive him of anything, he was about to deprive him of his liberty.

But in that thought, Devon was to find, as she hurried back along the hall and into the dining room, she had never been more wrong.

'I thought you'd prefer it if I let you be the one to see Grant out,' said Charles Johnston, and he was positively beaming as he witnessed her heightened colour.

Something's wrong somewhere, she thought. He wasn't looking remotely flattened. 'Er—Grant was in here with you for a long time,' she fished, and thought for a moment, as her father looked briefly away, that he was going to be evasive.

'He was casting an eye over the work I've done so far,' he told her equably after a moment. Then his broad grin was not to be restrained, and he was beaming again, too overjoyed himself to see that she was trying to hide her amazement when he followed up with, 'As soon as I've got this little lot cleared up, I'm to take myself back to my old office.'

That night in bed, Devon cried. She told herself it was just relief from tension that had been with her ever since her return from Sweden. But she knew that it wasn't. Grant had been far more magnanimous than she had thought. Without charging her to settle that outstanding debt, he had told her father to complete the project he had been engaged on, and that though he had re-thought the idea of a new plant, it would be of great interest to him to see how a fresh mind had tackled the problem.

She wept again as she recalled her father saying, that alive look in his eyes, 'I told Grant I should have my calculations completed by the weekend. And he said, as if it was the most natural thing in the world to say, "A week on Monday should see you back at your old desk, then,

Charles." And when I just looked blank, he shook me by the hand, and said, "You've suffered enough, man".'

Oh, Grant! she wept, and loved him more. She should have known him better, and she hadn't. She should have seen from just the way he had been, from the way he had made her rest, even as she had objected to being wrapped in cotton wool, that bitter though he might be about her father breaking that trust he and his father had placed in him, there was a kindness in him that redeemed his harshness.

Her mind was so full of Grant that night, she got up the next morning not totally surprised, even though she did admit to its being slightly unbelievable, that not once had she dwelt on her visit today to Mr McAllen.

Always before, a visit to her consultant had seen her spending a sleepless night. But though admitting now to feeling a twinge of apprehension, last night she had been too consumed with Grant to even remember her pending four o'clock appointment.

Her father joined her in the kitchen for lunch. And, when he rose to return to his endeavours, fully expecting him to say something to the effect that he would wrap things up at three so he could get ready to go with her to the clinic, when he did not, she had the impression, when she had so much proof of the extent of his caring, that he had forgotten all about it.

'I'll be off at about quarter past three,' she said by way of a hint. And then as he shuffled his feet, she could have sworn he looked uncomfortable. Suddenly she saw the reason why. 'I'm a big girl now, Dad,' she said, and was smiling as she added, 'Do you mind very much if I go on my own?'

He looked at her, his face grave, then after a pause, quietly, sincerely, he told her, 'I want what you want, Devon.'

She kissed him then as she told him to get back to his fusty old papers, for the reason why he preferred to work rather than go with her on her last appointment had just occurred to her. She felt indebted to Grant, and he too felt that same feeling of being in debt to him, only in his case because he could not repay him, he wanted to waste no time in getting stuck into Grant's work.

The words 'repay him' were in her mind the whole time she waited for her turn to see Mr McAllen. That same apprehension that had awakened with her was growing, and mingling with thoughts on the debt they owed Grant. Correction, she thought—the debt she owed Grant. For if Mr McAllen told her what she wanted to hear, then it was Grant who had forked out and paid for her to be a whole woman, and not, she saw clearly now, the withdrawn apology for a woman she had been on the way to becoming.

'Hello, Devon,' said Mr McAllen easily, when, clutching nervously at her bag, she eventually went in to see him. 'Let's have a look at you, shall we?'

She was elated as she swung away from the consulting rooms, Mr McAllen's, 'I don't expect you'll be sorry not to have to see me again,' still in her ears, the way it had been when his examination was over, his questions over.

'You mean,' she had said chokily, 'I don't have to come again?'

He had smiled, aware of her being strung up. 'You're as good as new,' he told her. 'Dr Henekssen did a first class job on you, Devon—you have a lot to thank him for.'

One of her first jobs, she thought as she walked on, was going to be to write and send Dr Henekssen the best 'Thank you' letter he had ever received. Mr McAllen was right, she thought, as she came to a park, the bright flowers growing there in abundance in tune with her mood calling her in; she did have a lot to thank him for.

And not only him, she thought, as she went over to a
bench and sat down. Mr McAllen too. And her father—
never would she be able to repay him, not only for his
years of caring, his years of always putting her first, but
the last and final most gigantic thing he had done for
her—sacrificed his integrity.

Love was in her heart for her father, but gratitude and
admiration for his courage were there too. For it must
have taken a tremendous amount of courage to have done
what he had done, wrong though in the eyes of the world
that act would appear. It must have cost him dear to have
done it, but had it not been for Grant, it would have cost
him so much more.

She had known it would not take long for her thoughts
to come around to Grant. But, whole again, knowing from
Mr McAllen's words that she was whole again, Devon
knew that there was one very big 'Thank you' outstanding
to Grant.

She owed him, yet he did not want payment. His words
about her eagerness turning him off were etched in her
soul. And yet last night, there had been that look of fire in
his eyes again when he had told her, 'When you look like
that I'm sorely inclined to forget my principles.'

What principles had he been talking of? Was it—a
fluttering inside her had to be controlled before she could
get her thoughts straight—was it as she had challenged
him once, that he would take no action to get her to
complete their bargain until after she had seen Mr Mc-
Allen? All of a sudden Devon's thinking took off in all
directions.

How long she sat there being pulled first one way and
then the other, she had no idea. She was on a see-saw she
couldn't get off, and she was growing more confused the
longer she thought about it. There was one very big thank
you owing to Grant, but that was getting mixed up with

thoughts on her own integrity, thoughts that she owed him more than a thank you, countered by thoughts that their bargain had been rendered null and void by what he had said to her. And anyway, as she remembered his bossing her about—but only when she thought about it, in the interests of getting her to rest—how could she go to him and tell him that the Johnstons always paid their debts? And did she want to? Though, if she was being so high-minded about wanting to settle with him, what did whether she wanted to have anything to do with that dishonourable debt?

Her insides churning, Devon left her bench and left the park, her mind still full of Grant and the debt she owed him. Her head no clearer, she found she was in that part of town where if she went one way she would be going in the direction of her own home, and if she went the other way she would be going in the direction of the home she had shared with Grant.

I love him, she thought, and without her having to think further, her feet had moved off in the direction of The Limes.

For the rest of the way, Devon tried to freeze all thought. She felt mixed up enough without going all through the thoughts she had had again. She owned she was so confused that she had no clear idea what she was going to say to Grant when she saw him. And she wasn't at all sure why she was going anyway, other than that something inside her seemed to be compelling her to go and see him.

She checked her watch when she had made it to the avenue where Grant lived, and was shattered to see it was half past six. Mr McAllen had been overrunning as usual, and that had made her late going in to see him, but surely she hadn't sat in the park all that time?

One thing, though, she thought, feeling faint inside, by

her arriving at Grant's house at this time of day, there was a very good chance that he would be in.

Doubt, uncertainty, knowing one careless arrogant word from him could have her wanting to die from embarrassment, Devon turned up the drive of The Limes, and felt anti-climax. Grant's car was not there—Grant was not there.

Why she kept on going she could not have said; too mixed up to think of turning about, she was able to reason later, she kept going forward. And she even rang the door bell once she had mounted the steps.

That no one answered was a foregone conclusion. But still she didn't seem able to move away. Stubbornness was with her not to admit defeat, not after she had got this far, for she knew with conviction that if she did not see Grant today, then she would never see him, because never would she have the nerve to come here again.

She had been standing on the wide doorstep for some five minutes with still no sign of Grant returning from work, when she suddenly remembered she had a key to the house in her bag. And her memory started to awaken through the fog of her thoughts, so she remembered that her father would be at home and, by this time be starting to get worried that she hadn't arrived.

That seemed to settle the matter for her. Depending on traffic, her father could have another three-quarters of an hour worrying about her before she could make it back.

The front door open, she walked through into the sitting room where she knew she would find a phone. But having dialled her home number, when her father answered and she had told him that she was fine, and that Mr McAllen had told her Dr Henekssen had done a perfect job on her, she realised she was not so clear of the fog that enmeshed her as she had thought. For she had not a clue what her father was talking about as he said something incomprehensible about there being a 'foul-up' before he went on to ask:

'Where are you phoning from, Devon?'

She had put the phone down after saying goodbye to him, before it dawned on her how scrambled her thinking had become. And she stared mortified at the instrument as she wondered what her father would be thinking, for as her words bounced back at her, she realised she had told him, 'I'm at Grant's home.'

Her legs feeling suddenly weak, she sat down and made herself concentrate on getting herself together. And at the end of ten minutes, she felt more composed, and able to comprehend that with her spirits never higher at Mr McAllen's good news, consumed by her love for Grant as she was, consumed by a need to see him—she had been making excuses to see him when, quite simply, she had wanted him to be the first to hear her good news. Which just went to show, she thought, how all over the place her thinking had been; for she had quite overlooked the fact that, in her need to share her news with the one she loved, she had forgotten completely that the one she loved did not love her!

Hurriedly she got to her feet, her thanks and gratitude to Grant relegated to letter form. Speedily she moved across the sitting room carpet, feeling hot at just the thought of what Grant would have to say if he came in and found her, as nice as you please, taking her ease on his settee.

She made it across the hall, and outside the front door. And then the roar of a car being driven fast and furiously up the drive had her turning, the front door still open behind her, and then, promptly, she froze.

The car had stopped, and as she saw Grant leap from it and come striding up to her, she did not have to wonder what he would have to say on returning from work to find her making free with his home. For his whole thunderous expression said it all, before he took the steps two at a time, grabbed her by the arm, and nearly shattered her eardrums as he bellowed:

'What the bloody hell are you doing *here*?'

CHAPTER ELEVEN

THAT Grant was in a rage such as she had never seen him in before made her quail where she stood. All too clear was the fact that he was deeply offended at her cheek in coming to his home and then having the effrontery to let herself in. Equally obvious, too, was the fact that he might have desired her at one time, but with or without principles, Grant Harrington had no time for her now.

'I was—just leaving,' she said, and took a step away from him, only to find, as his grip tightened on her arm, that she was going nowhere until he said so.

'Like hell you're leaving!' he snarled.

And in case she hadn't got the picture, the next second Devon found she was being manoeuvred back through the door she had just come through. And while she guessed she was in for a dressing down at her audacity in gaining entry and making as free with his home as if it were her own, she was being dragged after him.

Not another word did he have to spare for her until he had pulled her round, and they were standing facing each other on the sitting room carpet.

Telling herself she wasn't afraid of him even if his dark eyes were glinting dangerously, she tried to get herself together to think up some excuse for being there. But she was to find she had no time. For, looking as though he could cheerfully choke her, Grant was pitching into her, though to her astonishment, not taking her to task for treating The Limes as if it was a lodging house. But he had her staring at him witless, as he roared:

'Where the blazes have you been?' And, not giving her

chance to reply or question, 'You should have been home an hour ago at least!' Then, too angry, as uncomprehending of why that should cause him to be so infuriated she continued to stare, he thundered, 'And don't come the innocent blue eyes with me! You've given us one hell of a fright by not going straight home.'

'F-fright?' she queried, wondering how she had thought she had been confused before. Then she was trying hard to grasp what it was he was saying. 'Us?' she asked.

'Your father and me,' he bit, his jaw jutting pugnaciously as he let some light into her darkness.

'You've been—to my home?' she asked faintly, dearly wanting to sit down, but the mood he was in, guessing he would have her hauled to her feet for doing so uninvited.

'I was there when you eventually condescended to phone through,' he tossed at her.

'I'm sorry,' she said, her insides all of a flutter, hoping an apology might go some way to cool the heat of him as it registered that he must have driven like a madman to have got from her home and to The Limes so soon.

'So you damn well should be!' he blasted her, no let up in his aggression as he flung at her, 'We were worried sick about you.'

'Worried?' she dared to query, her heart's erratic pumping making her feel breathless.

'We thought you must have had bad news about your hip,' he said, searing her with a look.

Was Grant saying that he, as well as her father, had been worried about her? Her breath catching in her throat even as she discounted it, she found her voice to state, 'I'm—er—sorry if—er—if y . . . if anybody has been worried. But there was no need—I'm—er—fine. Mr Mc . . .'

'We know *that*,' he barked. 'I rang the clinic when you didn't arrive.'

'*You*—phoned?' she choked, her palms starting to grow moist. And she was then on the receiving end of his irritated look.

'I was all for coming to look for you,' he said grittily, 'but your father was of the opinion that you could appear at any moment from one of half a dozen routes.'

'You were going to come to meet me?' she exclaimed, her surprise overriding that he still wasn't looking too well pleased with her.

'I'd have blasted well taken you to keep your appointment,' he retorted impatiently, 'had you not told me your father was going with you.'

'Oh,' she said, thinking from what she could remember of his offer, it had only been if he could spare the time from his office. Though, on the defensive, she felt obliged to explain, 'He would have come with me, only—well, with the paperwork he was doing for you being so important to him, he . . .'

'*Nothing*,' Grant flattened her, 'is more important to him than you are.'

And before she could rush in to tell him that he didn't have to remind her, that they both had unsurmountable proof of that, he was going on to make her more confused than she already was, by saying:

'Do you think paperwork or anything else would have stopped him from going with you today—if it wasn't that your happiness means so much to him?'

Desperately Devon tried to make sense of that, and failed. 'But I don't understand,' she had to confess. 'He didn't argue when, seeing how involved he was with the work he's doing for you, I told him I wanted to go on my own.'

'Of course he didn't argue,' Grant said sharply. Then he paused, and looked exasperated suddenly. 'Oh, sit down,' he told her edgily.

Devon sat in the seat nearest to her, which happened to be the settee, more she thought because some of his aggression seemed to be fading, but that there was no saying it wouldn't be on the rampage again if she didn't comply with his order. Grant followed suit and claimed another part of the large settee, and either because she had acquiesced or because the first flash of his temper was over, she thought his voice was sounding more level as he said:

'Your father didn't argue with you because . . .' He stopped then as though choosing his words, when before he had thrown words at her in the heat of fury without caring. 'Your father thought,' he resumed after a moment, 'from the—discussion I had with him last night—that if I was not exactly going to take you to your appointment, then he was damn sure that I'd be meeting you from it.'

Panic hit her on the instant. 'You haven't told him about our bargain?'

'Oh, for God's sake!' and she had thought his fury had left him! 'To hell with any bargain we made!' he roared, making her jump.

'There's no need to shout!' she flared, her own voice rising, pride soaring. 'I heard you the first time when you said you'd gone off wanting me.'

'Dammit, woman,' he shouted, his voice none the quieter, 'of course I want you! Wanting you has been driving me bloody barmy!' Her heart threatening to leap from her body, Devon swallowed as he went on, 'But I didn't tell your father about the pact we made, simply because . . .'

'Because you thought he would sooner go to prison than have me give myself . . .'

Devon broke off as Grant's hands clenched, and she looked likely to be on the receiving end of one of those fists as he strove for control. She saw his hands uncurl, and her breathing became a little easier when, his hard-won control showing in that his voice was no longer a roar, but quiet and almost even, he said:

'Because I knew you didn't want him to know any of it.'

That took her aback for a moment. She recalled his astonished look last night when she had told him to 'Shut up' when she had thought her father might hear what he had been saying about them living together. She knew full well it was in him to tell her father everything, and she could only love Grant more that because he knew she did not want her father to know, he had kept quiet.

'Thank you, Grant,' she said huskily. And remembering that was not all she had to thank him for, she excused her calling at The Limes first before going home, 'I wanted to thank you personally for . . .' she faltered as she recalled she had been ready to leave without thanking him. 'I—was going to—write to you to—to thank you for . . .' she faltered again, her skin going pink as it struck her—he had not actually volunteered the money, had he? '. . . for—er—providing the money for my operation,' she made herself finish. 'For not prosecuting my father.'

'To hell with the money,' he said, dismissing the thousands of pounds he was out of pocket as if it were nothing. And when her eyes were fixed on his face, quietly he dropped out, 'Perhaps I should tell you that your father never was under any threat of being prosecuted.'

'Never was . . . ?' she gasped. But she just could not believe that. 'But you . . . When I came to your office . . .'

'When you came to my office I was amazed that after the years of loyal service your father had given both me and my father, anyone should think, even as shaken as I felt by it, that I could do that to him.'

'But . . .' She was still staggering.

'But,' he went on, 'shaken as I was, bitterly disappointed as I was, angered as I was,' he admitted, 'when maybe with another employee I wouldn't have taken such a personal interest. Because of my father's friendship and my own respect for your father, I had to find out why.' He broke off, then paused for a moment, and went on, his look severe, but, she was glad to see, his anger with her seemed to have gone, 'I have a—certain experience of life, so to my mind the money he'd stolen must either have been spent on gambling, or on some woman.'

'You—chose the latter,' she put in quietly.

'The latter chose me,' he said, unsmiling. 'I went to see him. I pulled up outside a small detached house that was well within your father's salary range. I observed a car standing on the drive that shouldn't have broken the bank even had it been this year's model. And my thought then was that he'd turned to gambling. That was,' he went on, 'until I saw those suitcases in the hall, until I saw you, beautiful, looking as though nothing in life had ever been denied you, a look of greedy anticipation in your eyes, I thought, as, too idle to shift yourself off the settee, you took your ease while your father looked about ready to collapse.'

'You—hated me on sight, didn't you?' she asked chokily.

'What I thought you stood for, yes,' he agreed. 'All I could see then was that regardless of how the father who had robbed for you fared, all you could think of was the good time that awaited you in Sweden. I couldn't bear to be in the same room with you.'

'Was that why you refused to see me when I came to your office?'

'I had no time for you,' he replied, but she had known that anyway.

Though when she was on the way to thinking that having thanked him, however inadequately, that the time had come for her to leave, and she glanced at him, there was that in his look that had her legs feeling watery again.

For, not taking his eyes from her, Grant was favouring her with a sort of—was it—a nervous expression? It couldn't be! And yet he looked to be a man with a lot on his mind, a man with a lot to say—and a man who, strangely for Grant, was not totally sure of the outcome!

Which was crazy, she thought, for Grant was always so absolutely sure of everything. She blamed what she thought she saw in him on her imagination. Hadn't she been so confused these past few hours as to have her thinking all over the place?

'I think I'd better go,' she said, and made to rise from the settee.

'No!' Grant said sharply.

And Devon was rapidly rethinking that he was in any way unsure of anything. For it was a decisive hand that came to her arm and pulled her to sit down again. And there was a firm control in his voice that belied the fact that he was in any way apprehensive—though it did nothing for *her* nerves to hear him state:

'To get back to that Friday—I did see you in my office, didn't I, Devon? And in consequence,' he said after a moment's pause. 'I spent the whole of the following weekend trying to get you out of my mind.'

'Oh!' she exclaimed, unable to hold the exclamation in. But her heartbeats evened out as she recalled how it had been. 'B-because you wanted me to pay,' she said. 'You had me on your mind because you were trying to think of a way to . . .'

'That's what I told myself, when wherever I went that weekend I was haunted by a pair of innocent-looking, pleading blue eyes, I didn't believe in.'

'Told—yourself?' she asked, and her heartbeats were erratic again when a slow smile came her way, and he owned:

'I didn't want to admit I was attracted to you.' And while she tried to make her heart behave, because she had to know he had been physically attracted to her or all of this would never have got started, he went on, 'That was why I phoned asking you to come to see me.' He shrugged self-deprecatingly. 'Of course when I saw you again, I had to admit to myself that I wanted you—but only, as I thought then, in a sexual way.'

Pink coloured her skin, but she rather thought it was more from the fact he had said 'but only, as I thought *then*' rather than the fact that sex had been brought into it.

'You'll forgive me, Devon, I hope,' he said, his mouth curving warmly as he observed the sudden pink of her skin, 'but I've been around sufficiently to know that there are such women as I first thought you were. It occurred to me then that I could kill the two proverbial birds with the one stone—have you living with me and hating it, thereby making you pay in some small measure for a change. And, for my part, having possessed you, I was sure living with you would soon be showing what I with my profound wisdom knew was false—that you were nowhere near as innocent as you were pretending. I was arrogantly positive that within days I would soon be seeing plenty in you not to admire.'

Her hands went damp at the thought—was Grant saying that he had found something in her *to* admire? She couldn't ask.

'But—you didn't—possess me,' she said huskily.

'How could I?' he questioned. 'For a start, I was in shock. You were, according to my superior intelligence, a girl who liked nothing but a good time. And yet there you were with a long and recent scar that couldn't be a lie—the proof that you'd been telling me the truth staring me in the face. The proof that, far from having a good time, you must recently have suffered terrible pain. Pain which, as something clicked in my head about you saying you were not to overstrain yourself, I saw you could know again if I couldn't get myself under control.'

'You did leave the room rather quickly,' she murmured as she remembered.

'It was touch and go, I don't mind telling you,' he said, a hint of a smile there that quickly disappeared, as he recalled, 'By morning, of course, even with the evidence of my eyes, I was back to thinking that you just couldn't be everything you were showing yourself to be.'

'Was that why you were bad-tempered with me sometimes?'

'Sometimes is probably an understatement,' he said. 'I still wanted to possess you, but wasn't liking it at all that you,' he paused momentarily, then added, 'had started taking possession of me.'

'I—possessed you!' Her eyes went wide as she stared at him, confused again, until he clarified, and had her throat going dry:

'You started to possess my head,' he explained ruefully. 'You were there with me everywhere I went, at home, at my office, in everything I did.' And while she swallowed painfully, 'So much so,' he said, 'that one day I found myself picking up the phone and dialling this number, for no other reason than that I just wanted to talk to you— God knows what I would have said had you answered.'

'I—didn't know it was—you,' she said chokily, knowing she had told him that before, but grasping for something to say, for suddenly, her thinking, had gone haywire.

'And I can clearly remember another day, when I'd thought of little else but you, a picture with me of you resting your limbs in the garden. I raced to get through my work so I could get home the sooner, only when I did— you weren't there.'

Devon had to clear her throat again. 'That was the day I went home . . .'

'And I was so angry, with you, with myself, that I demanded you handed over your house key.' Grant's look was rueful again as he said, 'Not knowing you'd got a spare tucked away somewhere. God, I must have been unbearable, but I didn't want you anywhere but here.'

'Because you—wanted me—available, whenever you decided to—er—to make me comply with the terms of our contract?' she questioned, wanting it to be more than that, but not seeing how it possibly could be.

'I was still telling myself that,' he said softly. And gently then, as if he could just not stop himself, he moved closer to her, and set her heart thudding when he leaned forward and placed a kiss to the side of her face, before going on. 'Even when by that time,' he murmured, a hand coming to brush a stray strand of silky blonde hair back from her face, his touch making her quiver, 'I'd discovered, to my amazement, that I was not always lusting after your body.'

Devon fell to earth with a bump. 'I remember,' she said, tears wanting to spurt, because for a few moments she had actually started to believe that Grant was saying that he had been on the way to caring for her in some small way. 'Your—preference—f-fell for a more experienced woman sometimes, didn't it?'

His arm coming round her shoulders as her words fell between them was something she could do without if she was to get herself under control. But her head shot round, as with her eyes glued hypnotised to his she heard him say, and sound sincere as he said it:

'I haven't looked at another woman since that day you struggled here from the bus stop with your cases, my dear.'

'But you told me . . .' she began, gasping at what he had said, at that softly murmured, 'my dear'.

'I said I wasn't always lusting after you, and that is true,' he broke in. 'There were many times when all I could think of was that I desperately wanted to protect that body that had known injury and pain, and was still healing after surgery. But,' he said, 'there were other times, times when—you'll forgive me—you were blatantly inviting me to take you. And those were the times when I had to get out of the house. Though not to go to another woman, as I led you to believe, but because I wanted you so badly, I couldn't be at all sure, had I stayed home, that I wouldn't be giving in and making you mine.'

Devon considered what he had just said. He had to care for her a little, didn't he? said her heart. Nonsense, said her head—when she did not want to listen to her head, but her head was not so easy to ignore.

'You say that you haven't looked at another woman, yet . . .' Oh God, it was coming out all wrong, she was actually sounding *jealous*! Devon decided to shut up.

'Yet?' Grant prompted, his look alert, nothing wrong with his hearing or his ability to pick up intonations, a smile quirking his mouth as he encouraged, 'Go on, Devon.'

'Well,' she said, picking every word carefully, 'that night, that last night, wh-when you told me to get into your bed—well,' she went on lamely, 'you went to—sleep.' His very silence had her going on, as she got deeper into the mire. 'I—th-thought,' she stammered, 'that it must be—because you had—had—er—used up your—er—excess energy elsewhere.'

The arm around her tightened, and he looked pleased about something—even as his smile fell away. 'I was furious with you for not being where I'd thought of you. As mad as hell when I came to your home and found you exhausted on the settee from labouring in your father's house, an overall wrapped round you, a kitchen full of home cooking—I was mad enough to want to frighten the daylights out of you,' he ended.

'But . . .' she began, recalling vividly how it had been, 'that still doesn't explain why you—went to sleep.'

'I didn't go to sleep,' he quietly shattered her by confessing. 'I let you think I was sleeping.' And leaving her with that to think on, he went on, 'I'd cooled off by the time I came to bed, and had a mighty argument with myself outside the bedroom door, then, because I hadn't seen you for two whole days,' he said, 'I couldn't take the single bed as I know I should have done, but came and joined you. When I was sure you were asleep, careful not to wake you, I took you in my arms, and felt near to content at last. I drifted off to sleep,' he concluded, 'and didn't waken until you stirred.'

'You were awake before I . . .' she gasped, starting to colour.

'I knew before you started kissing me that I had a battle on my hands,' he replied, revealing that he had awakened when her hand had touched his naked chest, and smiling at her blushes as she recalled how she had kissed him not once, but twice. 'But I still thought I was strong enough not to make love to you—I hadn't intended to—I just wanted to hold you. Your kisses weakened me, Devon,' he told her softly.

'But you didn't—make love to me,' she said, her voice gone husky again. 'You said you'd gone off me be-because I was throwing myself at you.'

His short bark of laughter told her that she had not been anywhere as near forward as she thought she had been.

'Which just goes to prove that I'm a better liar than I accused you of being,' he said, not looking at all abashed, as he confessed, 'The only reason I told you that, Devon

Johnston, was because after what had happened up there in that bedroom, I was back to wanting you like hell, yet I had no idea if when you saw your consultant, he might tell you you needed to give that hip another couple of weeks' rest. You,' he said quietly, 'had revealed that you wanted me as I wanted you, and I was convinced by then that we'd gone too far to go back to the way we were. I was desperate,' he owned. 'I sent for your father, and then you came downstairs and started arguing. Another few minutes of arguing on that subject, and I wasn't sure I would be waiting to take you upstairs before I gave in.'

Her throat seemed to have gone permanently dry, but as he came to an end, Devon managed, 'So you—attacked my pride by saying you'd—gone off me.'

'Which worked,' he said, but added with some charm, 'though you can soon prove me a liar.'

But Devon was not charmed. She was confused, she admitted that, for she had been on the way to believing that Grant really did have some caring for her. But what he had just said only went to prove how ridiculously wrong she had been.

'You . . .' she choked, and at the stricken look in her eyes, all humour left his face. 'You still want me to . . . Now that you know that my hip is—completely healed, you're saying that you want me to—to move back in to repay . . .' She broke off as she saw she had aroused instant anger in him.

'Oh, for . . . !' he started to explode, then he had himself under control, and asked tightly, 'Haven't you been listening to a word I've said? Didn't you hear me say forget the money? Didn't you get the message that there is no outstanding debt?'

Stubbornness took charge of her. She had let her heart believe he cared, but she must not listen to her heart again, but only to what her head was telling her.

'You want me to move back here with you?' she challenged.

'Yes, I want that,' he admitted. 'I . . .'

'Which is the same,' she cut in, her stubborn chin tilting, that or give way to a storm of weeping that she had been such an idiot to think he cared, 'the same,' she repeated, 'as saying that the debt is still out . . .'

'*Shut up!*' Devon blinked at the violence of the two words Grant threw at her. 'Shut up and listen,' he went on more quietly, and waited only to see that she hadn't a thing to say as she stayed quiet and looked ready to listen, before he went on to absolutely astound her, by saying, 'You're the first woman I've ever said "I love you" to—so perhaps I've done it very badly.' And while her heart selected a rhythm she was a stranger to, and she had thought she knew them all, he went on, 'I love you more than I ever knew it was possible to love, Devon Johnston. Thoughts of you consume me night and day. So much so that there've been times when I thought I would go crazy with it.'

'You—love me!' she gasped, forgetting in her shock that he had told her to shut up.

'My God!' he exclaimed, exasperated. 'What the hell do you think I've been telling you this past half hour if it wasn't that?'

'I—er . . .' she licked dry lips. 'I was—hoping it—what you said—meant that you—cared,' she managed after a struggle—and heard that Grant had picked out one word from the rest.

'Hoping?' he queried. Then suddenly his harsh look had gone from him, and a smile was creasing his face as he asked, 'Was I right to think I saw a look of love in your eyes for me? Was I right when I thought I heard a strain of jealousy in your voice?'

His smile was shortlived, and had disappeared altogether, tension taking him as Devon fought an unexpected shyness and tried to formulate her words. But in the end, as his face went from smiling to being stern, as if he was a man bracing himself to hear the worst, all she was capable of giving him was a straight answer.

'No, Grant,' she said, choked up inside, 'you were not—wrong.'

In the next second both his arms had come around her. 'And you love me?' he asked. 'Even though I've given you little cause to do anything but hate me?'

Her voice was barely audible, but he heard it. 'I love you, Grant,' she said breathily.

His name was the last word heard in the room for some time as Grant pulled her against him. Then he pulled back to look into her face, to look into her love-filled eyes. And then he was swallowing hard, and holding her close for long moments where she gulped convulsively. Then he was pulling back once more to look at her as if he just didn't believe any of it, and finally he kissed her.

Together they lay on the settee exchanging kisses and caresses. 'My darling, sweet Devon', he murmured at last, his hand moving up from her throat to the side of her face. 'Is it any wonder that I adore you? You're all the dear sweet innocent things I never believed you.'

Their lovemaking had been heated; she was as eager as him to get close, the buttons of her dress were undone, as were the buttons on his shirt. 'I'm feeling less and less innocent by the moment,' she said softly, and heard him laugh in delight with her.

'We still have some way to go,' he hinted, his other hand trailing the naked curve of her breast.

'Oh, Grant,' she sighed shakily. 'When you touch me like that, I'm not thinking any more.'

'Which leaves me,' he said, manfully taking his hand from the hardened peak he had created, and moving it so that his two hands cupped her face, 'having to think for

the two of us.' He smiled down at her then, as he confessed, 'Which also makes me think we'd better sit up if
I'm to try to think in any ordered pattern.'

With his assistance, Devon moved to sit beside him,
Grant not saying another word until with regret in his look
he had tidied first her clothing and then his own.

'Now,' he said, unable to resist just one more kiss on her
inviting lips, 'where was I?'

'Er—I think you were going to do some—er—ordered
thinking.'

He grinned, and as her heart flipped, so did Devon, her
lips managing to look inviting again. 'Cut it out,' he
growled, but he was looking so happy Devon had to laugh
from sheer joy. He looked away from her as if to get his
head clear, but he had his arm around her as he said:

'Much as I would prefer you spend tonight under my
roof, I think I should be doing something about ensuring
you have an early night in your own bed.'

'Yes, Grant,' she replied, too much in love with him,
knowing that he loved her, to object to anything he said or
did. Though since she had that day been pronounced
perfectly fit, she thought she ought to mention it. 'Why an
early night tonight especially?' she asked. 'I know it isn't
usual for a girl to hear her heart's two desires in one
day—one that she's as fit as any other girl, and the other,
that the man she loves,' she looked at him shyly, 'loves
her,' she said, 'but . . .'

'It isn't so usual either,' said Grant, his eyes loving
every inch of her face, 'for a girl to get engaged one day
and married the next.'

'*Married?*'

'You have no objection to our getting married tomorrow, I hope?' he asked, a touch tentatively, though not
looking ready to accept a refusal.

Hurriedly she shook her head. 'No, but . . .' she

answered, trying to think coherently, '. . . but—doesn't it take three days to get a—a special licence, or something?'

'I've had a special licence for longer than that,' he told her, watching her eyes pop in amazement. 'But with you being adamantly determined you wouldn't marry until you had your final all clear, loving you as I do, I thought it was the one thing I could do to let you know how much I loved you. I've made myself wait until this day.'

'Oh, Grant,' she whispered, and just had to lean forward and kiss him.

Their kiss lengthened, and threatened to get out of hand. Then suddenly Grant was pulling back from her, trying to tease, for all he seemed to be searching for some of the control that had been abandoned.

'You kiss me like that tomorrow night, my girl, and see where it gets you,' he said ruefully—and pulled her to her feet and headed her towards the door.

'Come on, witch,' he said, 'let's get out of here and back to where your father is waiting.'

'My father!' Devon exclaimed, feeling suddenly guilty that for so long she had forgotten him. 'I've no idea what he'll say about . . .'

'Us,' supplied Grant, moving her more slowly out into the hall. His grin appeared as outside the front door they stood on the wide top step and he locked the door behind them. 'I don't think you'll find him too surprised. I told him last night that I was going to ask you to marry me today.'

He went to go down the steps, but moved back to her side when he felt her resistance as she stood rooted and stared. 'You didn't!' she exclaimed.

'Why do you think he didn't go with you today?' he asked. And as she stood and gaped, he kissed her, and looked delighted at her stupefaction, as he told her, 'He told me when I went round to wait for both you and him, as I thought, to return from your appointment, that knowing I wasn't one to let the grass grow, he was positive I would be meeting you from the clinic. He was certain I would propose to you then and there.' And as Devon stood goggling, he gently urged her across the top step. 'Shall we go and tell him our good news, my darling?' he asked.

'Good news?' she echoed, still stunned.

'You will marry me tomorrow, won't you?' he asked gently.

What could she reply? Only what was in her heart. 'Oh yes,' she said, her face alight with love, laughter and happiness bubbling up. 'Oh, Grant,' she sighed, 'I love you so much, tomorrow can't come soon enough!'

On the top step of his home, Grant took her in his arms and held her very close. His voice was thick, his kiss on her brow, when it came, a benediction, as gently he told her:

'All your tomorrows are going to be happy, my dearest love, I promise you,' he vowed.

Harlequin Plus

A WORD ABOUT THE AUTHOR

Jessica Steele's father was a railwayman from Worcester-shire, in west central England, and her mother came from the valleys of Wales. She herself was born in Leamington, a city in the English Midlands. She was sixth in a family of seven children, and her close-knit home life helped her immensely in the long battle against severe ill health that she waged as a child and young woman. She was more than thirty before she decided to write something other than the poetry she had been composing for her own enjoyment. It took her some time and several rejected attempts before she produced a manuscript that was accepted for publication—but she was aided in her efforts by two things: her own stubbornly determined spirit and the vigorous encouragement of her second husband, Peter.

She says, "What a joy it was when that first acceptance came through! Peter mopped me up, and neither of us cooked that night—we went out to dinner."

Now that she's a full-time writer, Jessica is able to travel farther afield than previously. She has visited such exciting places as Hong Kong, Mexico, Malta and Japan, all of which form fascinating backdrops for her many Romances and Presents novels.

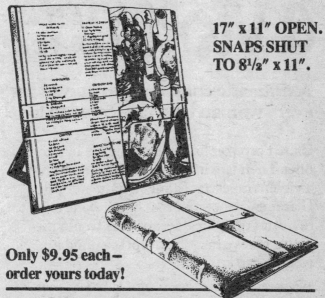